The power of a whisper...

Once Leslie had settled in next to Randy, she was amazed at how comfortable it was to sit on the floor. The gentle warmth from the fire and the sated feeling within her allowed Leslie to relax more than usual. For the first time she let her guard down completely and enjoyed a companionable moment with Randy.... It was not until Leslie suggested she be going that he made an attempt to touch her.

"Not yet," he pleaded, reaching out and gently caressing her cheek with the palm of his hand. Warm shafts of delight coursed through her. "Leslie, stay a while longer."

"I have to work tomorrow. Not everyone gets Saturdays off, you know." But she was concentrating not on what she was saying, but on the sensitive touch of his hand. This time she did not pull away from him.

"Please stay," he said in a near whisper. "Please."

ABOUT THE AUTHOR

Rosalyn Alsobrook's writing career began at age three with a "book" she wrote for her father in eighteen words, one to a page. Her dad gave it rave reviews. Much later in college, she wrote a how-to column on auto mechanics. She gathered the information firsthand by working as assistant manager in an auto-parts store. Rosalyn lives in Texas with her husband, two sons, five cats, two frogs and a pet lobster.

Books by Rosalyn Alsobrook

HARLEQUIN AMERICAN ROMANCE

All or Nothing

ROSALYN ALSOBROOK

Harlequin Books

TORONTO • NEW YORK • LONDON
AMSTERDAM • PARIS • SYDNEY • HAMBURG
STOCKHOLM • ATHENS • TOKYO • MILAN

To my son Andy,
who is already a teenager
To my son Tony,
who is already in first grade
But especially to my husband,
Bobby,
who makes me feel young in spite of it all

Published May 1985
First printing March 1985

ISBN 0-373-16103-4

Chapter One

What else could go wrong? There had to be an end to it. First there was that notice of the delayed shipment on all those toys that had already been included in this week's sales circular, then came the mixup at the bank, which had bounced several of their checks. That had promptly been followed by the plumbing problem in the ladies' rest room on the top floor. Then, just before closing time the day before, the new computer malfunctioned, just two days out of warranty, and Leslie had been the one forced to stay at the store until nearly nine while servicemen worked on the problem.

After everything that had gone wrong that day, Leslie Lovall was in no mood to start out the next morning with a fresh set of problems. She felt she was rapidly coming to the end of her rope. This just might be the straw that broke her.

"It's now ten minutes after eight," Leslie pointed out, glancing down impatiently at her gold wristwatch for the fifth time in the past ten minutes. She had hoped to get to work early to help process the sales that the computer had missed while it was down, but now it looked as if they just might have to be late instead.

Having always prided herself on being punctual, Leslie grew more irritated with each passing minute.

"I know," her mother responded with a ladened sigh, wishing Leslie had not appointed herself time-keeper.

It was times like this that made Margaret Lovall wonder what had happened to the sweet, fun-loving person her daughter had been before having had the family business thrust at her. Margaret felt partly responsible that Leslie had slowly changed from a cheerful, easygoing young girl in college to a somber, serious-minded businesswoman in just a few short years. Even Leslie's appearance had changed drastically.

Before, Leslie had always worn her long dark-brown hair in soft, flowing styles, but now she had shoulder-length hair worn back in a loose but unadorning bun, and she usually dressed in practical business outfits like the pale-blue three-piece outfit she had on today, even when she was not working. Although Leslie was still unmistakably pretty, her makeup was always at a minimum, whether she was dressing for work or not, and she selected only simple, although expensive, jewelry.

"She's late," Leslie went on to complain.

"So you've told me."

"Well, she had better have a very good excuse," Leslie warned as she poured more orange juice into her small glass, thinking her mother should be more concerned than she was. Leslie had learned from experience that an employer had to have a firm hand when dealing with employees or should expect to be taken full advantage of.

"I'm sure she will," Margaret told her daughter, shaking her head, clearly wishing Leslie was not taking this matter so seriously. "The housekeeping service I chose has a very good reputation. It's the same service Virginia used, and you know how wonderful her housekeeper is. Besides, I checked them out thoroughly before placing my name with them."

"If she isn't here very soon, I'm going to call that service," Leslie said firmly, setting her juice down before she had taken even a sip. "Are you sure that this is the right day? Maybe you misunderstood and she's not due to arrive today at all."

"Yes, I'm certain of it. I'm sure something unavoidable has delayed her. Calm down, for heaven's sake — she'll probably be here any minute. No sense hanging her before she's had a fair trial."

"I just hope she doesn't plan to make a habit of being late. It's not the sign of a good, trustworthy employee. She could at least have given us a call. I can't remember Lucille ever being late without at least giving us a call."

Margaret could not argue that point.

Leslie was right about Lucille. In the eleven years that Lucille Thomas had been their housekeeper, she had rarely been late. She had been a good and conscientious employee from the start, and while they both hated her having to leave them, they knew it simply could not be helped. Lucille's daughter, who had recently been in a serious automobile accident, had been left partially paralyzed, and Lucille was planning to move to Pennsylvania to be with her. She had repeatedly expressed her regrets to Margaret and Leslie for having to leave, especially with the holidays approaching, but her priorities had to be with her daughter, who would be getting out of the hospital any day now.

Margaret had been quick to agree that Lucille's place was with her daughter, and had not encouraged Lucille to stay on in Shreveport. She fully understood; after all, she was a mother, too, and had begun searching for a competent replacement immediately. Lucille had agreed to stay just long enough to show the new housekeeper around and explain the duties, even though Margaret had been put on a three-week waiting list in order to receive full-time help.

Leslie felt they were losing a part of the family. If Lucille's replacement did not show up soon, with a good reason for being late, Leslie intended to see that this was the new housekeeper's last day. It infuriated her that the woman had so little consideration. It was nearly time for Leslie and her mother to leave for work. They could not afford to wait around much longer. Leslie sat sipping her orange juice while her mother went upstairs to get her purse. Leslie really hated to leave before having a word with the delinquent housekeeper, but she also hated the thought of being late for work herself. After all, the boss was supposed to set an example for the others.

Lucille had brought in the newspaper but Leslie was so irritated by the new woman's tardiness that she could not concentrate on her reading. She continued to glance down at her watch every few seconds. It was now eight-fifteen; the woman was supposed to have been there at seven-thirty.

When the door chimes finally sounded, Leslie quickly pushed back her chair and tossed her napkin on the table in a wadded heap. As she rose hurriedly from her seat, she called out to Lucille and her mother, "I'll answer it."

The chimes sounded a second time before Leslie could make her way through the entry to open the front door, which infuriated her even more. Why, all of a sudden, was the blasted woman in such a hurry?

"Coming," she shouted as she marched briskly toward the door, feeling the hem of her linen skirt snap against her legs. She fully intended to let the woman know just how she felt about her being forty-five minutes late, and on her first day. Having dealt with this kind of employee before, Leslie knew she had to be stern. She was not going to be taken advantage of; nor would she allow her mother to be. They were not going to put up with such thoughtlessness, and this woman might as well be warned of it from the very start.

Leslie started her speech even before the door was fully open. "You're late! You were supposed to be here at exactly seven-thirty!"

"I know, and I'm sorry, but the service wrote your address down wrong. For some reason, my requisition says East instead off West Briarwood, and I ended up heading in the wrong direction. When I reached the location and found this same street number on the front door of a vacated building, I had to locate a pay phone so I could call in to find out what the deal was. I do apologize, but it shouldn't happen again. I'm usually early, if anything."

Leslie's golden-brown eyes grew wide, and she was momentarily unable to reply. She was so stunned by

the appearance of the person before her that words
failed her miserably. The smiling face greeting her did
not belong to a neatly dressed mature older woman as
she had expected, nor was it the face of a primly uni-
formed younger woman. To Leslie's amazement and
dismay, she was not facing a woman at all. Instead, she
was being greeted by a young man—a very attractive,
virile-looking young man of about thirty.

There were no two ways about it. Although there
seemed to be a faulty connection between her brain
and her mouth at the moment, there was nothing
wrong with her eyes. There definitely was a man standing before her. And she noticed that nothing seemed to
be wrong with his eyes, either. In fact, they were the
most uncanny shade of crystal blue she had ever seen,
and they were sparkling expectantly at her. She realized
he was waiting for her to say something—after all, it
was her turn to speak. Still slightly stunned, she managed to locate her voice and break the awkward silence.
"Who are you?"

"Randy Brinnad, at your service." He clicked the
heels of his tennis shoes together like a butler in an old
movie, but since he was wearing canvas shoes instead
of hard-soled ones, the action seemed rather ridiculous.

"At my service?"

"I'm your new housekeeper," he informed her with
a brisk nod. As he stepped inside to get out of the cold,
he reached around to his hip pocket and slid a folded
piece of paper out of his noticeably tight blue jeans and
handed it to her as soon as she had closed the door.
While Leslie slowly unfolded the paper, finding it oddly

disconcerting that the paper felt so warm to her fingers, he began to unsnap the front of his waist-length denim jacket, quietly viewing the interior of the entry and trying to get glimpses of other rooms through open doors. While his interest seemed to lie with the house, Leslie took a moment to look him over. Although not so devastatingly handsome that women would have to stop what they were doing to stare mindlessly, he was strangely attractive.

There was something about this Randy Brinnad that made him worth a second look. Maybe it was those unearthly blue eyes laced with long dark lashes, or maybe it was his lightly curling, sandy-brown hair. Although thinning slightly at the hairline, his hair was styled so its thinness seemed more of an asset than not. It also wasn't his height that demanded another look; he was only about four inches taller than her own five feet seven, no giant hulk by any means. He wasn't even powerfully muscular, yet he looked fit, and the muscles his tight jeans displayed certainly seemed well toned. There did not appear to be any excess anywhere.

Pulling her gaze away from him, Leslie read over the work requisition and was more than a little bemused by what she read. It certainly seemed legitimate enough. This man had actually been sent over here to be their housekeeper. As she refolded the paper abruptly, the annoyance she felt quickly spread across her face. "But you can't be the new housekeeper, you're a—you're a—"

"Man?" He finished the sentence for her.

"Exactly. You are a man."

"Very observant, I must say." He grinned easily,

showing a double set of long, narrow dimples. Looking down at himself with a critical eye, he commented further, "I think you might be right. I don't have enough curves to be a woman." Looking back at her, he smiled a wicked, gleaming smile that made her take a step back. His crystal gaze traveled away from her face for just a moment. "Now you seem to have all the right curves in all the right places. I'll bet you are a woman."

"Sir!" This was the last straw. No matter how good-looking he was, she did not need him or his impudence.

"Call me Randy. My other employers did." His voice was low and masculine, smooth as silk.

"You're not exactly what we had in mind when we called your service for a housekeeper. I'm sorry, but I really don't think you're quite right for this job."

"Because I'm a man?"

"Exactly." She waved her arms for emphasis. "This job is not at all suited for a man. We need someone with experience keeping the place spotless, running errands, managing the meals. The house is old and requires special care, and we are very particular about our meals. We also need someone who can take care of personal errands, like shopping and going by the cleaners when necessary."

"And you don't think a man is capable of doing all that," he said, in more of an observation than a question. The smile had faded from his face, but his mellow voice did not yet reveal his anger.

"Not as capable as a woman would be."

"Why is that?"

"Because a woman is used to doing such things."

"I assure you that, even though I'm unfortunate enough to be of the male gender, I am fully capable of keeping a house in order as well as cooking nutritious meals, and I can also hold my own in a supermarket."

"But we were expecting a woman."

"Why?"

"Why?" she repeated in exasperation. "Because, Mr. Brinnad, housekeepers are supposed to be women."

"And why is that?"

"They just are. It's just the way things are. It's tradition." Placing her fists on her narrow hips, she tried one last time to explain. "In all my life, I've never known a man who could adequately take care of himself, much less try to take care of someone else." Her own father had been a prime example. Although able to run a large business with no trouble, the man would not spread mustard on his own sandwich without first calling her mother into the kitchen to help him, and he probably wouldn't have known the difference between floor polish and furniture wax—and really wouldn't have cared that there was a difference anyway.

"Well, I'm sorry you feel the way you do. Actually, I think I would have been just the person to see to your needs—and I'd have enjoyed doing it." As he took a step toward her, the wicked gleam returned to his crystal eyes. "If you would just return my requisition, I'll be on my way, Mrs. Lovall."

"*Miss* Lovall—I'm not married," she informed him, handing him the refolded piece of paper.

"Oh? It said here 'Mrs. Lovall.'"

"That's my mother."

"You mean you are not Mrs. Margaret Lovall?" Renewed vigor was in his voice—maybe all was not lost.

"No, I'm Leslie. Margaret is my mother."

"Then you really have no right to dismiss me, do you? You aren't the one who wanted to hire me in the first place. Where is your mother? I'd like a word with her."

"I don't think that will do you any good," Leslie told him, angered that he had not accepted what she'd had to say on the matter and gone quietly. She was not at all pleased at his obstinate nature.

"Still, I would like a word with Margaret Lovall."

"I'm Margaret Lovall" came a voice from behind them. They both turned to find Margaret smiling graciously, headed in their direction.

Leslie opened her mouth to speak, but before she could, she found Randy Brinnad introducing himself to her mother.

"Hello, I'm Randy Brinnad, the one Bellamy's House Care sent over. I'm sorry I'm late, but I was given the wrong address."

Margaret's smile grew, practically overwhelming her gentle face, as she greeted the handsome young man. She had overheard the terse conversation between the two, and had liked the way the young man had held his own with Leslie. Not many people ever got the upper hand around her formidable young daughter, and it looked as if this man was well on his way to doing just that. "You are going to be my new housekeeper?"

"I certainly hope so." He smiled back at her, causing his dimples to reappear. Leslie, feeling he was laying the charm on a little thick, was convinced her mother would see through him in a minute. "But there may be a problem."

"Oh? And what might that be?"

"Me. I don't know if you noticed it or not, but I'm not a woman. I hear you might not be willing to give a man a chance at the job."

Leslie stiffened. He was mocking her.

"Nonsense, I see no reason why being a man would create a problem. In fact, I love the idea."

"Mother—" Leslie started to interrupt, but Margaret was not paying attention to her. Instead, she had turned and called for Lucille.

"Mother, don't you think a woman would be more suitable?" Again, Margaret ignored her while she read the requisition papers Randy had handed her. It was obvious that she had already accepted the idea of having the young man as their housekeeper, but Leslie waited until her mother had finished reading before she tried one more time. "Mother, do you really think it's wise to hire a man to be your housekeeper?"

"What difference does it make as long as he does a good job—and judging from his references here, he does a very fine job. Besides, I have all those parties to get ready for. I was on a three-week waiting list before I was able to get anyone full time. I can't afford to wait another three weeks for someone else, and if I was to accept temporary help, I might end up with a different person every day, and each one would spend half the time trying to find everything. Besides, I'm certainly too busy to do the work myself—and so are you, what with the Christmas rush and all. I need the help now, and as long as he does his job, I see no reason why I shouldn't hire him. Besides, I think he's kind of cute.''

"And I do windows.'' Randy smiled broadly. He was clearly amused.

Even Lucille was quickly taken in by Randy's charms and escorted him willingly to the kitchen to start familiarizing him with the house. She had agreed with Margaret that it would be quite a novelty to have a male housekeeper. Leslie was obviously outvoted. Angrily, she snatched her coat from the tall brass clothestree near the door and marched out to wait for her mother in the car. The pompous ass may have gotten the upper hand this time, but she would see that it didn't last. The man had to go.

Leslie would have preferred to make the trip to Lovall's in total silence, but her mother talked incessantly about how the world was always changing, using male housekeepers for her main example of the change. Leslie felt that that was the trouble with the world, it was always changing. Just when things seemed to be going well, something happened to turn things around. By the time Leslie had parked and the two of them had stepped inside the building, she was more than looking forward to a few quiet hours in her office, burying herself in her work and putting all thoughts of the changing world far out of her mind.

Pausing a moment at the door that led into Margaret's office on the second floor, Leslie waited until her mother had stepped inside and had bid her farewell before turning to leave. As always, her mother's last words were, "See you at one.''

"Okay, Mother, see you then,'' Leslie called out over her shoulder, already headed toward her own office down the hall. It really was not necessary for Margaret to remind Leslie that they would see each other at one. Unless an emergency arose or Leslie had planned a business lunch of some sort in town, the two of them always went home together at one for a light meal. Margaret usually stayed home for the rest of the afternoon while Leslie would go back to work, not returning until five or later on most days.

It was the routine they had fallen into ever since her mother had decided to come to work part-time. Leslie was glad that she had finally taken an active part in the business, although she now realized her mother would never take her rightful place as head of Lovall's. Six years ago, when Leslie had dropped out of her third year of college to take over the business soon after her father's fatal heart attack, she had thought she was just taking it over until her mother could pull herself together and learn the business. Although she had intended to work for the family business eventually, Leslie had hoped to finish college first and enjoy a bit more of her youth before having such responsibilities placed on her.

The responsibilities had been more than Leslie had originally anticipated. Having been unable to cope with her husband's death, Margaret had neglected the business for several months before finally turning to her daughter for help. Leslie's father had been one of those take-charge men who had always done everything for himself, leaving no one else in a position to take over at his death. He had not even trained anyone to be his assistant, so when he died, the employees had immediately looked to Margaret for guidance.

Once confronted with the problem, Leslie had readi-

ly come to the rescue, but it had not been easy for her.
She had only had two and a half years of business
courses to aid her when she sat down with the accountant that first day and discovered for herself that the
business had been steadily losing ground. Lovall's Department Store had been showing a loss for almost a
year, especially during those last few months after her
father's death, when, essentially, there had been no
one managing the business. The employees had continued to fulfill their duties in an effort to keep the business going as best they could, but with no person truly
in charge, their situation had gone from bad to hopeless.

Leslie had immediately set out to discover why business had dropped so drastically, and she soon realized
that it was due to the public's growing interest in the
new malls and shopping centers in the area. Interest in
all the large department-type stores in the downtown
district had fallen. She'd decided that their last chance
to compete would be to lower their prices and become a
discount store. She'd instigated a huge advertising cam-
paign promoting new lower prices and same high quality, and it proved to be a sound decision.

Gradually, Lovall's Discount Center began to pull
itself out of debt. Leslie had saved not only the business but the family home as well, because her mother
had seriously been considering selling the house to
help meet towering expenses. But now that Lovall's
was geared toward dealing in high volume, the business
was doing exceptionally well, and there had been no
more talk of selling the house. Financial problems were
once again a thing of the past.

Despite the fact that Leslie had once assumed that her reign as head of Lovall's was only temporary, having expected her mother eventually to overcome her grief and take over, Leslie did not really resent the work. Every time she walked into her outer office and was greeted by her own personal secretary before heading into her private inner office, Leslie could not help but feel a certain pride in herself. In all honesty, she enjoyed the challenges and met each head-on. Yesterday had only proved again that she was quite capable of handling any emergency that arrived, but still it irritated her when she had to handle emergency upon emergency upon emergency. There was only so much she could tolerate, and lately it took less and less to make her lose her temper.

Trying to put all her problems and aggravations out of her mind, including a certain insufferable Randy Brinnad, Leslie sat down at her desk and began her routine of examining the daily reports from the different departments and combining them into one overall report. She was glad to find that her always-efficient secretary, Cassie Haught, was already busily inputting all the sales the computer had missed yesterday while it was down. Leslie would be able to concentrate on her usual things.

With Christmas just around the corner, sales were up in every department. Leslie found two requests on her desk for additional employees from the heads of both the sporting goods and housewares departments. Glancing at their sales records for the past five days, she decided the requests were legitimate and called Cassie into her office. As always, Cassie was there in a matter of seconds, unperturbed about her interrupted work.

"Cassie, I want you to send these request forms to Andy in personnel, along with a memo asking him to find seasonal help for both these departments. Then you need to send both Ken, in sporting goods, and Shirley, in housewares, messages that their requests have been granted."

Reaching out to accept the papers Leslie was handing her, Cassie asked, "Did you get a chance to sign those insurance papers I filled out yesterday? The insurance company is sending a man over later this morning to examine the damage in the top-floor ladies' room and pick up the forms."

Sagging noticeably, Leslie sighed. "I took them home with me last night to look them over. I also carried a copy of the policy home with me. I wanted to see how much of the damage I could expect them to take care of."

"And you left them at home," Cassie concluded, shaking her head with concern. "It's not like you to be as forgetful as you have been lately. I think you're working too hard. It wouldn't harm you, and the world wouldn't collapse, if you let me take care of more of your duties."

"No, you do enough as it is," Leslie stated firmly, smiling at the young girl who had been her secretary for almost two years now. Cassie had a way of knowing what needed to be done even before Leslie had a chance to tell her. "Actually, I don't think overwork has anything to do with it. I think it's old age setting in a little prematurely."

"At twenty-seven? I hardly think so. Do you want me to run by your house and get the insurance papers for you? They really should be here when the insurance man comes by for them."

"No, that would throw you way behind, and I'd rather not go myself. I'll see if Mother has time to go by there." Leslie pulled the phone closer and picked up the receiver, quickly punching out the number of her mother's extension. When there was no answer by the sixth ring, Leslie finally hung up and asked Cassie to see if she could find her mother and tell her about the needed insurance papers. As soon as Cassie left, Leslie returned to the pile of messages on her desk. She was still returning calls when Cassie slipped quietly back into the office.

Aware that Cassie was playing with the ends of her long blond hair, Leslie knew that, heaven help them, something else had gone wrong. Finishing her conversation with the loquacious salesman from a firm she had never even heard of, Leslie slowly replaced the receiver and took a deep breath.

"Okay, Cassie, what's wrong? Did Mother say she'd be unable to get the insurance papers for me?"

"No, she said she would gladly see to it."

"What then?"

"Santa Claus just slipped in the rest room and may have broken his leg. They had to take him to a hospital."

"No Santa Claus?"

"And lots of children waiting to see him."

"Call Andy in personnel and see if we can get a replacement in a hurry. Never mind, I'll do it. We have to have a Santa. Lovall's is famous for its Santa's Workshop.''

Snatching up the phone, Leslie punched out Andy's extension number, then reached gently up and massaged the back of her neck while she waited for the phone to ring. Desperately, she tried to remain calm. Closing her eyes, she willed Andy to have someone to replace their Santa—immediately.

Andy answered the phone on the second ring.

Once Leslie had explained the situation, she wanted to know if there was anyone to take over the job, the sooner the better.

"I'll have to check through my files and see if any of the seasonal applicants are able to go right to work. Surely I can find someone. I'll call you back when I do.''

Despite her confidence in Andy Edwards, Leslie worried about the vacant Santa's chair while she opened the mail Cassie had just left on her desk. She hated to disappoint the children who looked forward to sitting on Santa's lap and telling him just what they hoped to get for Christmas. By the time Andy called back, she had decided they would have a Santa if she had to go down there and be Santa herself.

Andy had managed to find one who would be able to start work later that day but he wouldn't be able to be there until at least two. That meant there wouldn't be a Santa for the next three hours.

"Is that the best you could do?"

"Afraid so. Do you want me to hire him?"

"Go ahead," she said broodingly, feeling somehow defeated. She had hoped Andy would know of someone who could come right away.

As soon as she hung up, she called Cassie back in and ordered her to bring a Santa Claus suit to her office pronto. She offered no explanation and Cassie asked for none as she hurried out of the office to do as she was told. Ten minutes later, she brought in a large unopened package.

"I had to get a suit out of stock. The man who broke his leg wore his Santa suit to the hospital," Cassie explained when she placed the large box on Leslie's desk.

"Thank you. This is fine," Leslie assured her, then waited until Cassie had returned to her desk in the next room before getting up and quietly closing the door. Moments later, she reopened the door and walked out of her office as Santa Claus. Nodding to her stunned secretary, she offered a few ho-hos before heading out into the hall. Just before disappearing from sight, she turned back and told Cassie to warn her mother that they would not be going home until at least two o'clock.

As she made her way downstairs to the toy department where Santa's Workshop was on display, she was feeling rather cocky. Another problem solved. If she just remained calm and tried to reason things out, she could solve just about any problem. It suddenly occurred to her that if she just put her mind to it, she would be able to think of a way to take care of a certain Randy Brinnad as well. The thought of that warmed her to her very soul. Underneath her snow-white artificial beard, Leslie was all smiles.

When she reached the toy department, she was instantly swarmed by a wide assortment of eager kids. Tony Allen, the head of the toy department, came over to get the new Santa squared away. Fighting his way through the throng of children, he began directing them to the area they were supposed to go to to wait in line. When he had finally maneuvered all the children away, he turned and sighed with relief.

"Am I ever glad to see you," he exclaimed, extending his hand in greeting. "We've only been without a Santa for an hour, and I'll bet I've had a hundred complaints. I'm Tony, the big kid in charge of toys. Since Andy didn't call and tell me you were coming, you'll have to tell me your name."

Leslie smiled, knowing what a shock it was going to be to the man. "My name's Leslie Lovall. Ever heard of me?"

Tony's mouth opened slightly in amazement. "Miss Lovall? Our boss?"

"The same. Now if you would quickly brief me on exactly what it is Santa does here, I'll get to work."

Suddenly seeming nervous, Tony motioned to the huge, brightly painted chair that greatly resembled a king's throne and explained, "All you really have to do is to ask the children if they've been good or not and then ask them what they want for you—er, Santa—to bring them for Christmas. If they don't seem to know, you suggest things their mothers can buy here. Then before they leave, you give them a balloon and a piece of candy out of your sack, which is hidden in a compartment under the chair."

"That doesn't seem too difficult," Leslie commented, glancing at the eager line of kids.

"It's not so difficult as it is tiring and nerve-racking. How long do you plan to be Santa?"

"Just until two, when the replacement is due to arrive. I think I can last that long. Actually, I think I might actually enjoy this."

"We'll see," Tony mumbled below his breath so Leslie was barely able to hear it. Then, in a much stronger voice, he added, "If you decide you need a break, signal me and I'll place the 'Santa Will Be Right Back' sign behind the last kid in line."

"That last Santa must have taken you literally when you told him he could have a break," Leslie commented, referring to the condition of the man's leg, but when Tony did not catch the intended humor, she shrugged and headed for Santa's throne.

It only took a couple of minutes to locate the bag with the candy and balloons and get situated in the seat. She adjusted the towel she had wadded up to give her a paunchy stomach, then signaled for Tony to let the children start coming.

The first was a boy about five years old, a skinny, freckle-faced little boy with long, curly black hair and sparkling green eyes. In his eagerness to speak to Santa, he ran up to the platform and, in two large, bounding leaps, landed right in Leslie's lap.

"Hi, Santa!"

Taking a moment to recover from the blow, Leslie patted him on the head and coughed out a few ho-ho-hos.

"Aren't you gonna ask what I want for Christmas?"

Obviously, this kid was a pro at visiting Santa. Trying to make herself sound masculine, Leslie pulled in her chin, tightened her larynx, and spoke in as low a voice as she could. "Of course, little boy. What do you want for Christmas?"

Except for the Christmas music coming in over the intercom, there was a dead silence. The boy screwed up his face and peered curiously into her eyes. "You sure you're Santa?"

"Why, of course—why do you ask?"

"I dunno. You sound a little weird."

"Oh, that. I've been sick."

Wiggling back and forth on her knees, he nodded his agreement. "Yeah, you must have been real sick. You've lost a lot of weight, too. You sure got knobby knees."

Worried now that the boy was about to prove her a fraud, she decided to distract him by going ahead and giving him his candy and balloon. Having singled out one of each, she tried to hand them to him.

"But I haven't told you what I want yet."

Leslie was tempted to tell the kid to write her a letter, but instead she asked calmly, "And do you know what you want for Christmas?"

"Sure I do. I want a G.I. Joe gun, a sno-cone machine, a big truck, lots of cars and a alligator."

"An alligator?"

"And a G.I. Joe gun, a sno-cone machine, a big truck and lots of cars."

"A live alligator?"

"Well, a dead one wouldn't be much good." He shook his head as if he couldn't believe Santa was this dumb.

While Leslie stared down at the boy and wondered what he intended to do with a live alligator, the child tilted his shaggy head and asked her if she had got all that.

"Oh, certainly. And if you're a good boy—" of which she had serious doubts "—I'll see what I can do about getting you what you asked for."

The boy, narrowing his eyes, stubbornly refused to get down when she gave him a gentle push. In a very suspicious voice, he asked, "Just how are you going to know who to give these things to? You never asked me what my name is."

Leslie stammered a moment before finally deciding to run the risk of a bluff. "Oh, I don't have to ask you your name. I remember you from last year."

The boy considered that a moment, then, as if he'd decided that Santa probably would remember him, he hopped down and started to leave, with his candy and balloon in hand. Just as she was about to wave the next child on, the boy turned and demanded she prove that she did indeed remember him. "What is my name?"

"Jeff," she replied proudly, silently praising the pure genius of whoever had thought of personalizing the back of little boy's belts, and smiled gratefully as the little boy finally left. She motioned for the next child to come up.

For the next hour, Leslie was visited by a steady stream of children of all shapes, and sizes and ages. She had to deal with the flirts, the criers, the wigglers, the gigglers, the fiddlers, the overly curious babblers and the strong, blissfully silent types. As the time wore on, she began to wonder what they paid Santa—whatever it was, she was absolutely certain it wasn't enough. She was going to check into it and make sure that Santa got what his job was worth.

With a little over an hour down and an hour and a

half to go, Leslie began to watch in earnest the huge wall clock behind the toy department register. Would two o'clock never get here?

Suddenly her eyes were drawn to a man, standing only a few feet away, whom she hadn't noticed before. He was leaning against the North Pole and grinning at her like a cat who had cornered himself a tasty little mouse. Although she had seen him only one time, earlier that morning, she recognized him immediately. It was that insidious Randy Brinnad, and he seemed extremely pleased and amused about something.

Chapter Two

Lazily, Randy pushed himself away from the candy-striped post brightly labeled "North Pole" and nodded to Leslie by way of greeting. His self-confidence was obvious as he stared at her with those celestial blue eyes of his. She wasn't sure how he knew, but she realized he was fully aware who was behind all the white hair and red velvet. What in the world was he doing here, anyway?

Leslie noticed that her heartbeat felt like tiny explosions in her chest and that her stomach seemed to be trying something new and acrobatic deep inside her, but she attributed the strange sensations to the fact that it had startled her to find him there at all, when he was supposed to be at her mother's house, involved in learning about his new job.

Then it occurred to her that perhaps he'd decided he didn't want the job after all, that he might have come to resign. If that was his reason for being here—and what other reason could there be?—she decided she'd be extremely gracious about it and offer him a week's severance. She'd try to refrain from reminding him how she had warned him at the outset. It simply wasn't a job for a man.

While she was thinking of how graciously she'd deal with the matter, the next child approached her and climbed shyly onto her lap. Looking down at the little girl, Leslie could feel Randy's penetrating gaze still on her. Why did it bother her that he was watching her? Since she was Santa, lots of pople were staring at her openly, and some were even pointing—why should it matter now that one more pair of eyes were on her?

Trying not to think about Randy for the moment, knowing she would deal with him when she finished with the little girl on her lap, she asked the child what Santa could bring her for Christmas, then tried earnestly to listen to the girl's lengthy reply. When the child finally finished, was presented with her candy and a balloon, and had left with a glowing smile, Leslie glanced back in Randy's direction, only to realize that he had moved even closer to her. He was now standing on the edge of the platform, right next to her chair. If she were to be so inclined, she could have reached out and touched him. For a brief moment, she actually thought she wanted to. How ridiculous!

"Really, my dear, I don't think you're quite right for this particular job," he began, talking in a low voice so that only she could hear the mellow sarcasm that enveloped his words. "Somehow I've always thought of Santa as being a man, and, as I clearly recall, we established earlier this morning that you are definitely a woman. You do remember, don't you? Me—man, you—woman? Excuse the pun, but don't you think a man would be better suited for this job?"

"And what difference does it make to you?" she asked, crossing both her arms and legs defiantly, causing her pillowed stomach to paunch out between them. Unaware of how ridiculous she looked, she glared into his pale-blue eyes while she waited for his reply, knowing in advance that she really didn't want to hear a word he had to say. Almost every time the man opened his mouth, something irritating came out—and this time proved to be no exception.

"I have Santa's reputation to consider. In all my thirty years, I've never once thought Santa could possibly be a woman. He's always seemed more like the kind and gentle grandfatherly type to me. Now I've considered the possibility that Mrs. Santa is female, but never once have I felt that Santa could be a woman."

Placing his fists on his hips in an effort to mimic Leslie's earlier stance, he added, "As I said, I do think a man would be much better suited for this job. After all, it's tradition." Lazily crossing his arms across his chest, he shook his head disbelievingly, looking as if he were disappointed in her. "And I was under the impression that you were a strong believer in tradition and that you had clear and set ideas as to what a man's role in life should be."

"I'll have you know that we have a man coming in to take over in an hour," she informed him quickly, trying to keep her voice low, too. She didn't care to have all these children discover that the Santa they were looking at was a total fraud. "I'm just filling in until he can get here."

"Well, if you can be Santa, then why can't I be a housekeeper?" Although he was not exactly smiling, his crystal eyes were dancing with merriment, and Leslie found his obvious pleasure in the situation to be more than a little annoying.

"That's entirely different and you know it," she hissed, her dark eyes narrowing with her struggle to keep from screaming at his insolence.

"How is it different?"

"This was an emergency. We needed a Santa and couldn't spare anyone else to fill in. With so many shoppers these days, we have to have every available salesperson out there on the floor. In fact, everyone from the office staff to the stockboys is being over-worked right now. I was really the only one available at the moment."

"And just because you were available makes it all right? How come my availability doesn't make it all right for me to be your mother's housekeeper? After all, I'm at least qualified for the job. What experience have you had at being Santa?"

"Just what are you doing here anyway?" If he had come to tell her he was quitting the job, she wished he would just get to it and stop trying to provoke one last argument.

"Your mother called and asked if I would mind bringing some papers over for her. Since running errands is one of my new duties, I came right over with them. Just before I left her office, she told me to warn Lucille that you two would be arriving late for lunch because you were busy being Santa and wouldn't be able to break loose until around two. Having heard that, I had to come down here and see it for myself."

He was obviously trying to stifle a grin, and failing miserably. His dimples twitched with his efforts.

Aware that the man was still making fun of her, Leslie actually felt like hitting him. Being so tempted toward violence, she didn't want to continue the argument in front of the customers, especially the children. She was just about to signal Tony to put the "Santa Will Be Right Back" sign up for her when Randy pulled back his shirt sleeve and glanced at his watch.

"I'd love to stay and discuss this further with you, but I must be going. I'm only scheduled ten-minute breaks, and I dare not take a minute over that." He leaned forward and spoke as if he were confiding in her. "Although my new boss is a really sweet and understanding lady, she has a very spoiled and stubborn daughter who I think would just love to cause me a lot of trouble, so I have to watch my step."

Leslie did not appreciate Randy's poor attempt at humor one bit, and she was just about to tell him so when he spoke again. "Oh, and Santa, I don't think you should cross your legs at the knee like that. You're going to give Santa Claus a terrible reputation. It's bad enough you've got these kids believing Santa wears eyeshadow and perfume."

Exasperated, all Leslie could do was sputter in indignation while Randy casually strode away. In a way she wanted to laugh at the irony of the situation—after all, even she had considered Santa's job to be just as much a man's as being a housekeeper was a woman's—but the gall of that man! How dared he make fun of her and call her spoiled and stubborn! With more determination than ever, she knew she had to do something about him, and soon—she certainly did not need this kind of aggravation in her life. She had enough problems. How could she make her mother see him for what he really was, a sharp-tongued, egotistical troublemaker?

Leslie could hardly pay attention to what any of the children said to her after that. And when Tony came up to whisper in her ear that the new Santa had arrived, she could scarcely believe that another hour had passed. Tony placed the "Santa Will Be Right Back" sign behind the last child, and Leslie only had to listen to three more children before making a rapid exit through the nearest "Employees Only" door.

She hurried up to her office to change out of the suit so it could be sent down to the new man. As soon as she was back in her clothes and had a moment, she glanced through the yellow pages in an effort to find another housekeeping service; she wanted to replace Randy Brinnad, but she no longer trusted the service her mother had chosen. With her poor luck of late, they would just send her mother another man. How could they possibly imagine that a man could ever become a good housekeeper? What bothered her more was that her mother seemed perfectly content with the idea—although she would never have expected her father to so much as pick up his own newspaper. In fact, if housekeeping had been left to her father, the decor they lived in would have been Early Clutter. She needed to remind her mother of that.

Feeling more confident now that she would somehow manage to convince her mother to dismiss that horrible man, she went ahead and placed a call to

Creel's Housekeeping, leaving her name on another waiting list for full-time help. Her mother had been right about one thing—they did need help, and would want a replacement as soon as possible.

In a much better mood, she was just replacing the receiver when her mother entered her office.

"Are you ready to go, Leslie?"

"Just let me get my purse," she replied cheerfully. "Are you as hungry as I am? Suddenly I'm famished."

"Santa Clausing must be hard work," her mother commented, looking curiously at her daughter. She wondered what had brought on such joviality when Leslie had been so prone to rotten moods lately.

"You wouldn't believe..." Leslie said, laughing, then proceeded to tell her mother the many strange experiences she had had over the past few hours, but excluding any mention of Randy Brinnad for the moment. She would wait for just the right moment to speak with her mother about that. Maybe after an obvious blunder in his work her mother would be more receptive to complaints.

Moments later Leslie and her mother pulled into the driveway where Randy's bright-red 1934 Chevrolet coupe was parked. Noticing the golden-yellow flames painted along the sides, Leslie thought the car certainly matched the guy's personality—quite overbearing, to say the least. She couldn't help but notice the contrast when she glanced beyond the souped-up hot rod to her mother's beautiful, sedate home, and was certain she was doing the right thing in searching for more suitable help. Even his car didn't fit into their surroundings.

The dignified old colonial structure stood proudly

among majestic oaks and magnolias and blended well
with the other stately homes in the restored section of
Shreveport, Louisiana, where it stood. It occurred to
her that the people who had originally built this lovely
home back in the mid-1800s would be as appalled as
she was to have a man in charge of its welfare.

Six modified Doric columns supported the second-
story gallery while rising to meet the moderate cornice
that surmounted them. A major part of the house was
made of handmade brick that had been plastered and
painted white. The ornate balustrades along the upper
gallery had been painted glossy black to match the
heavy wooden doors and the huge shutters that had
stood guard for many years over the large windows that
ranged, equally spaced, across both floors.

Although always in the shadows of the mammoth
trees surrounding it, the house never seemed gloomy
or veiled. To Leslie, this quiet and serene setting was a
refuge from her hectic days at Lovall's. Although she
now had her own apartment closer to downtown, Leslie
still spent much of her spare time at her mother's, enjoying the peacefulness. It was a haven of sorts, and she
did not want to have it invaded by the likes of Randy
Brinnad or his souped-up car. Just thinking about it
made her hands tighten on the steering wheel until her
knuckles turned white.

Entering the house, Margaret immediately called out
to Lucille that they were home. Passing by the dining
room on their way upstairs to freshen up, Leslie noticed that Lucille had gotten out the Christmas linen
and had decorated the table with bright-red napkins
and matching tapered candles. She had also placed a

lovely arrangement of poinsettias in the center of the table. It was quite a welcome change.

Leslie realized that Lucille wanted this last day to be special. Feeling saddened by the thought, Leslie slowly made her way upstairs to wash her hands and tidy her hair, which was still mussed from the false beard and wig. While she worked to redo her hair, she found herself thinking about Randy Brinnad and their earlier encounter, and when she finally went back downstairs, she discovered she had much less of an appetite than before. Her mother, already seated, was lightly shaking salt on a large leafy salad. Taking her seat beside her mother, Leslie tried not to seem as annoyed as she felt. Right now, she simply wanted to enjoy the lovely meal and put Randy far out of her mind.

"Looks like Lucille has gone out of her way to make this last day special," Leslie commented, smiling at the thought of the woman's generous nature. "The salad looks great."

"It certainly does. And Lucille didn't spare any of your favorites. There's shrimp, eggs, cheeses, tomatoes, and lots of olives." Margaret paused and looked wistful for a moment. "I really hate to think of her leaving us."

And I hate to think of whom you've hired to replace her, Leslie thought, but aloud she said, "We'll miss her, that's for sure. Is everything set for the farewell dinner tonight?"

Leaning toward Leslie, Margaret turned to watch the door that led into the kitchen. In an almost soundless whisper, she answered, "Everything is go. Just you remember to stop by Bellotte's and pick up the present."

"What about the cake? Don't you want me to go by the bakery?"

"No, that won't be necessary. When I had Randy bring me the insurance papers earlier, I told him what we were planning, and he volunteered to pick up the cake and stay late to help. He's also going to try to keep Lucille out of the kitchen for me while I get everything ready."

"You've asked him to help? Why? We don't need him." Leslie frowned at the thought of his intruding on tonight. Tonight was special.

"I didn't ask him to help. I just told him what we were planning and he volunteered. He told me that Lucille has been very nice in explaining where everything was and has carefully shown him just how I like things done around the house. He said helping me with this would be a way to return the kindness she's shown him today."

Leslie reached up and slowly rubbed her temples in an attempt to remain calm while she thought this through. She didn't want to appear childish, but she also didn't want Randy to ruin the evening for her, and she was sure he would. She searched her mind for a way out of this without seeming like the stubborn, spoiled person he had claimed her to be, but for the life of her, she could not come up with a single idea. She could only hope that he wouldn't stay for the whole thing. Surely he wouldn't—he wasn't dressed for a dinner party.

Before Leslie and Margaret could discuss the evening further, Lucille and Randy entered the dining room, each carrying a steaming bowl of Swedish mushroom soup. Randy was also carrying a small basket of lightly browned finger rolls. Lucille placed the bowl she was carrying in front of Margaret, leaving Randy to place his in front of Leslie. Leaning forward over Leslie's shoulder, he placed the rolls on the table.

"Nice and warm," he commented. Then, before straightening up, he asked if there was anything they needed. Leslie became electrically aware that his shoulder was lightly pressing against hers, and for one maddening moment she could hardly breathe.

The heat of Randy's body seemed to sear right through both layers of clothing. Suddenly her senses whirled, and she was temporarily disoriented. Even after he stood back, she continued to feel the warmth against her shoulders, and reaction to their sudden personal contact confused her. She should have felt appalled or repulsed, but instead she felt strangely pleased, almost aroused. The feeling was a totally new experience for her, and she was not at all certain how she should label it. She only knew it was not at all the reaction she should have expected.

Having kept most of her relationships with men on a purely platonic level, Leslie had always been able to maintain complete control of her life, and was quite proud of the accomplishment. Although she enjoyed the companionship of her men friends, she had never allowed herself to get too serious about any of her suitors. But she had never led them on, either. She had always openly told them at the beginning that she was not at all interested in a serious relationship. Whenever anyone tried to get too personal, in any way, she would quickly withdraw and look for someone less aggressive to share what little time she had to devote to friendships.

Leslie had managed to remain true to her convictions. A romantic involvement would take up too much of the time and energy she needed for the business. And her father's business was extremely important to her. That's why she enjoyed relationships like the one she was presently having with John LaFerney. She did not have to stay on guard with him, and he never demanded more than an occasional evening from her. She felt safe whenever she was with John—there was no worrying about losing her identity or her independence. John had always complied with her rules and had never tried to become anything more than just a close friend. She appreciated him for that.

Leslie was determined never to let anyone trap her and hold her bound by her own emotions, as so many women did. Even her mother had allowed herself to become so emotionally bound to her father that she had been able to live only in his shadow, letting him tell her every move she should make. Other than those dealing with the household, she had never dared to make her own decisions. No such self-imprisonment for Leslie. She enjoyed her life-style too much to change it for any man. Tightening her fists, Leslie silently repeated her vow of independence. No, it would never happen to her. She would never allow any man that sort of control over her. She was too smart for that.

"I guess we have everything we need," Leslie heard her mother saying. Her mother's words brought her thoughts away from the odd sensations Randy's touch had provoked in her. "Lucille, you've really outdone yourself. The salad is delicious, and this table is lovely, so bright and cheerful."

"Thank you." Lucille smiled easily, glancing over at Randy and giving him a teasing wink. "But I must confess, Randy set the table and made both the soup and the salad. All I did was show him where everything was."

Leslie looked down at her soup as if it were poison. "Randy made this?"

"Indeed he did," Lucille exclaimed. "Wait until you taste it. It's delicious. I'm trying to wheedle the recipe out of him."

Leslie lowered her spoon carefully into the soup, letting it fill, then lifted it to her lips for a tentative taste. She was disappointed to find out that Lucille had been absolutely correct. It was delicious. Randy's being able to cook was going to make it that much harder to convince her mother to dismiss him. But then, soup was not usually that difficult to prepare. With any luck, he would be a complete washout when it came to preparing more complicated dishes.

Holding on to that last thought, she reluctantly agreed that the soup was very tasty, but she refused to look up into the satisfied gleam she knew she would find in his arrogant crystal eyes as she dipped her spoon into the soup again.

After asking once more if there was anything else they would need, Randy and Lucille went back into the kitchen. As they closed the door behind them, Leslie could hear Lucille trying to guess the ingredients that were in his mysterious soup.

"I think Randy is going to do just fine, don't you?"

Margaret asked before putting another spoonful of soup into her mouth. Savoring the taste for just a moment before swallowing, she closed her gentle blue eyes and moaned aloud with pleasure.

"No comment."

"Don't tell me you still believe he's unqualified simply because he's a man."

"It's still too soon to tell, don't you think? Just because he can make a tasty soup doesn't mean he will be able to do all the other things expected of him. I think in time you're going to find that I was right all along. I really don't believe he's going to work out."

"I've got a feeling he is going to surprise you," Margaret replied, looking oddly satisfied when she glanced back down at her bowl. She smiled as if she could see images of the future in its shallow depths.

Realizing that right now it would be no use telling her mother how horribly the young man had behaved to her, Leslie dropped the subject of Randy Brinnad for the moment. She realized that the best thing for her to do was to be patient and wait for him to make his first big bungle.

But bungling was not something Randy often did. He was not only capable but very competent, and right now he was wondering how long it would take Leslie to see that. Although eventually he knew she would come to realize his abilities—after all, the lady was no dummy—he was eager to hurry and win her over to his side. While he worked to learn all he could about his new job and his new employer, his thoughts kept returning to his new employer's sexy young daughter and the pertinacious way she tossed her head to prove a point and the way her dark-brown eyes flashed with anger whenever he said something that irritated her. It made aggravating her such pure joy.

Being way behind in her work did not seem to encourage Leslie to concentrate on business as it should have once she had returned to her office. Try as she might, she was unable to push disturbing thoughts of Randy Brinnad from her mind, and the more she thought about him the more confused she became. He was the most insolent, exasperating man she had ever met, yet when they'd touched, she'd almost melted in her chair. It just didn't make sense. She should have felt repulsed at having had physical contact with someone she loathed as much as she loathed him, yet her insides still tingled from the mere thought of it.

Still trying to reason it all out when the time came to leave her office, Leslie almost forgot to stop by Bellotte's to pick up the lovely coat they had purchased for Lucille as a reminder of how much they loved her. When Leslie pulled into the driveway and saw that the Chevy coupe was still there, she was a mass of mixed emotions. She was furious at the upheaval the man had managed to cause in her life in less than one day, yet somewhere, mixed in with all the anger and frustration, she also felt a tiny shiver of delight in knowing he was still there. She didn't need all this turmoil and confusion—she preferred her world to be as orderly and uncomplicated as possible—but as long as Randy Brinnad was around, she knew her life would be constant bedlam. He would destroy the only haven from her hectic days at Lovall's. Even her own apartment could not supply the peace and quiet she found here; indeed, at times she wondered why she had thought it so all-important to move out of her mother's house. And why had she ever chosen to lease an apartment instead of a house? She just did not fit into apartment living.

As she parked her brown Regency in the garage next to her mother's station wagon, Leslie realized that her decision to get herself an apartment had largely to do with Carol, her best friend. She and Carol had been friends since girlhood, and for some reason that always eluded Leslie, Carol had forever been able to get her to listen to her ideas, no matter how wild they seemed. There was just something in Carol's enthusiasm that always lured Leslie into doing things she wouldn't normally do.

If there was ever a perfect example of the saying that opposites attract, Leslie knew she and Carol were it. Carol loved to get involved, especially with men—and lots of them. In fact, Carol was in and out of relationships so often that Leslie had given up trying to keep up with them all. And whereas Leslie preferred quiet dinners and solitude, Carol loved to be out in a crowd. Leslie could never understand how Carol managed to meet new people so easily. There were no strangers for Carol, only people she had yet to meet. Carol was flamboyant and carefree where Leslie tended to be far more reserved. Carol was short and blond; Leslie was tall and brunette. Carol loved to listen to Bob Seger; Leslie preferred Lionel Richie. Leslie was usually very rational in making decisions, while Carol tended to be rather reckless. It was hard to imagine that an undying friendship could exist between the two, but exist it did. Although they hardly ever agreed fully on anything, they would defend each other to the very end. Mismatched as they were, they were an inseparable pair.

Knowing that Carol would be at the dinner tonight, Leslie wondered what her friend would have to say about Randy. She had a feeling Carol was going to be quite taken with her mother's handsome new housekeeper and just might want to add him to her long list of men. Carol had always been one to judge a man by appearances first, waiting until later to search for any redeeming values or something they might have in common.

At the thought of Carol and Randy getting together, Leslie felt a dull, clenching ache in the very pit of her stomach—a feeling she could neither understand nor explain, even to herself. When she had more time to dwell on it, she would be able to reason all this out, but for now she had to hurry upstairs and change. For some reason she wanted to look her best tonight.

Chapter Three

Leslie had hoped to be dressed and downstairs early enough to help her mother with the final preparations, but she was running late. Nothing seemed to be going right anymore. First she had not been able to find the lacy full slip she had wanted to wear. It had been moved. After she finally located the slip, she'd discovered a spot on the dress she had brought over earlier. She tried to wash it out with a dab of soap and the corner of a washcloth, but then she realized that the spot only seemed to be getting larger with her efforts. Finally she gave up and chose another dress from those she had left behind at her mother's because of the lack of closet space in her apartment.

Having to give up the dress she'd really wanted to wear only worsened Leslie's already dour mood. She had so wanted to look her absolute best tonight.

Laying the newly chosen dress across the bed, she hurried to put on her makeup. After taking great pains with it for a change, she started on her hair, which refused to cooperate fully, and when she finally did get the more contrary locks to look halfway attractive, she realized she was out of hairspray. Her thick and unruly hair would never hold shape without it.

"Give me strength," she mumbled aloud as she considered whether she should run down the hall to her mother's room to see if she had some hairspray or just put her hair up in a simple knot that would require no spray.

Deciding she would rather wear her hair down loose, Leslie hurried out of her own room and down the hallway toward her mother's suite. In her haste to finish getting ready in what little time was left, Leslie had forgotten all about the fact that there was a man in the house and had not bothered to pull her robe on over her scanty slip. When she padded into her mother's bathroom in her pantyhose and slip, she was so quiet that Randy did not hear her enter. It was her involuntary gasp that gave her away.

Looking up from where he was kneeling in front of an open cabinet, his crystal eyes widened with surprise. The carefully folded towels he was just about to put away dropped to the floor in a crumpled heap, where they lay forgotten. In appreciation of her lack of clothing, his sparkling eyes traveled the full length of her body while a devilish smile slowly spread across his face. His dimples deepened as the smile grew.

"That's some outfit you have on, Ms. Lovall." The glimmering blue of his eyes came to rest on the long shapely legs that were revealed by the short, clinging slip. Letting out a heavy breath, he formed the word "wow" with his lips.

"What are you doing in here?" she asked, trying to cover as much of herself with her two arms as possible.

Attempting to back out of her mother's bathroom and beyond range of his keen sight as quickly as possible, she bumped awkwardly into the edge of the door. To her chagrin, the jostled door promptly moved away from her, closing securely behind her with a deafening click.

"I was helping Lucille put away the clean laundry, but I'm nearly through with that and am presently open to any suggestions you might have. What exactly do you have in mind?" he asked with a sly lift of his brows, letting his gaze drift over her again. There was evil lurking in the depths of those crystal eyes, she was sure of it.

With a mock look of horror, Randy gasped innocently, then said, placing his hand over his heart, "Why, Ms. Lovall, are you planning to take advantage of me?"

Mortified, Leslie began to stammer. "Don't be ridiculous. I had no idea you were in here."

"You don't have to play games with me, Ms. Lovall, I wasn't born yesterday. I know that such things occur. Besides, I'm more than willing to cooperate." He grinned, his narrow dimples seeming suddenly wicked. Rising, he moved toward her with the agility of a cat. As he made his approach, a rakish smile on his ruggedly handsome face, his left hand went to the buttons of his shirt and his right hand went out to brace the door before she could reach for the knob. He had her trapped against the full-length mirror, the cold surface of which only seemed to sharpen her awareness of her predicament.

"I'm not playing games. I didn't know you were in

here." Did he really think that she had planned any of this?

"And as soon as you realized that I was in here all alone and helpless, you closed the door," he said softly, his warm breath falling across her cheek as he freed two of his buttons. "How very clever you are." With the top three buttons now undone, a generous portion of his chest was exposed, a view Leslie tried to ignore.

"Th-that was an accident. I didn't mean for the door to close," she replied. She realized her voice sounded weaker than it should have. Where was her usual sharp, decisive tone? She tried to clear her throat but found the effort to be totally useless.

"You mean you don't intend to ravish my body?" Randy sounded crushed. A boyish pout perched itself on his handsome face, and a new dimple formed in the cleft of his chin. "You aren't planning to take advantage of me?"

"Certainly not!"

Nowhere were their bodies touching, yet Leslie could feel his warmth just the same. The heat radiated through her body, and as the warmth spread, so did her anger. She was furious at his implication that she could have such calculated motivations, yet at the same time she found the thoughts he had provoked in her to be intriguing, almost worth stopping to consider. What would it be like to seduce this man? How successful would such an attempt be, anyway? She had never thought of herself as particularly alluring.

Everything inside Leslie seemed to be spinning in high gear. She was dealing with too many emotions at

one time. The anger that tore at her she understood,
but the wildly erotic sensations she was experiencing
were totally foreign to her, and they left her as confused as ever. Her heartbeat was out of control. Gazing
down, she was aware that his shirt front was still half
open, inviting her attention. There before her was a
beautiful mass of dark hair running softly across a muscular chest. Why the unexpected urge to reach out and
feel the texture? This sudden awareness made her an-
grier still, as much at herself as at him.

Finally her anger conquered the other emotions vy-
ing for control. "I told you, I never expected to find
you in here. I just came to get Mother's hairspray."

Having spoken, she reached out and gave him a determined shove, careful not to make contact with the
exposed skin, afraid touching him there would weaken
her hard-fought resolve.

"Well," he drawled as he stepped slowly back, his
lashes lowered just enough to make him look incredibly
sexy. "If you ever change your mind..."

"You are insufferable!"

"And *you* are beautiful—that is, what I see of you
certainly is."

That unexpected reply caused Leslie to pause, her
hand gripping the knob. She was just about to retort
that he might as well enjoy what he happened to see
now because he certainly would never be privy to the
rest when there came a light tapping on the door.

"Randy, are you in there?"

It was Lucille. Leslie closed her eyes for strength.
What was Lucille going to think if she saw her state of
undress and then noticed Randy's partially undone

shirt? How was she going to explain the closed door? Knowing this had all happened innocently enough, why did she suddenly feel so guilty?

"Yes, ma'am," Randy replied calmly, raising his voice so that he could be heard through the door. With irritating slowness he began to rebutton his shirt, turning away from Leslie. "I'll be right out."

Reaching down, he gathered the crumpled towels and carefully refolded them before placing them inside the cabinet. Leslie found that she was totally speechless as she waited to see what was going to happen. She was certain that Lucille, considering the incriminating evidence, would think the worst, and the thought of Lucille's disappointment in her made her heart ache. Her insides felt as if they were made of lead.

When Randy closed the cabinet door, he leaned over and flushed the commode. While waiting for the noise to subside, he strode back over to where Leslie still stood with her back plastered to the now foggy mirror. Putting his warm hands on either of her bare shoulders, he forcefully moved her a few feet to the left of the door and bent down to place a brief kiss on the tip of her nose.

His dimples lengthened as he whispered with uncontained mirth, "Remember, when you finally do decide you want me, I'll be more than willing to oblige. After all, I've already decided I want you."

Casually opening the bathroom door, an action that penned Leslie against a small closet door, Randy walked out, leaving the bathroom door open to shield her from view. Leslie remained behind the safety of the door for several minutes after she heard Randy and

Lucille's voices fade from the room. A fingertip went to the place his lips had ever so lightly pressed against the end of her nose as if to verify that he had, indeed, kissed her. The kiss had been so unexpected she wasn't sure it had happened at all.

A gentle warmth that seemed to originate at the tip of her nose surged through her being, causing her a mindless moment of pleasure, but when her brain quickly started to refunction, this was followed by an immediate blast of anger. She was overwhelmed by Randy's audacity and the total lack of respect he seemed to have for her. It was not proper for an employee to be so forward with his employer. Granted, her mother was his true employer, but he really should show her the same courtesies and respect.

"That—man," she growled, feeling he should never have behaved the way he just had. He had no right even to insinuate that she could possibly want him or that body of his in any way, especially when such an insinuation was so absurd. She could barely tolerate the man. He was a constant source of aggravation, and that ego of his was not to be believed.

Seething, Leslie realized she should have slapped his face when he had so boldly trapped her against the door and implied they could be intimate. Why hadn't she slapped him? He more than deserved it. And why did his parting words seem branded on her brain? His having told her that he wanted her made her suddenly tense with anticipation. What if he was serious about wanting her? She was not sure how she felt about that. Shaking her head, she decided the idea was too ridiculous even to consider. He had said he wanted her for the shock value it would have. He had an odd craving to see her speechless and defensive. It was all part of the game he seemed to be playing with her, a game she wanted no part of.

With clenched fists, Leslie eased the door back. Peeking around the edge to make absolutely certain no one was still in her mother's room, she stepped out slowly and carefully. Remembering the reason she had come, she snatched up her mother's hairspray and headed back to her room. Leaning into the hallway this time, to make certain the coast was clear, she noticed Carol standing just down the hall, staring in the opposite direction. Hurrying along, Leslie greeted her friend with a barely audible hello, without bothering to so much as slow down or nod. Curiosity aroused, Carol followed her on inside.

"Mind telling me who that good-looking guy was I just saw going down the hall with Lucille?"

Stepping in front of her mirror and retouching her hair, Leslie looked at her friend through the reflection. She responded to the question in a flat tone. "That was Randy Brinnad, Mom's new housekeeper."

"Say what?" Carol tilted her pretty blond head as if trying to decide whether or not she should consider having her hearing tested.

"The housekeeping service Mom chose sent that guy over here, and Mom hired him. He's her new housekeeper."

"You're kidding!" Carol sighed in open-mouthed amazement. Her azure eyes sparkled with delight over this bit of news. "How lucky can you get?"

"I'd say it was anything but lucky. The guy is bad

news, plain and simple." Leslie was letting her anger
show when she slammed the brush down on the dresser top. Grasping the hairspray and snapping the lid off,
she added, "That guy is nothing but trouble."

"You two had a run-in of some sort?" Carol wanted
to know as she lifted back the corner of the dress Leslie
was going to wear so she could sit down on the edge of
the bed. Crossing her short but shapely legs, she carefully spread her long, flowing cranberry-colored skirt
over her knees and waited eagerly for Leslie's reply.

"More than once. We seem to clash every time we
get near each other. It's like he loves to irritate me, but
then, maybe it's his way of getting even."

"For what?" Carol leaned forward, showing that her
interest was continuing to grow.

"I let him know right from the start that I didn't
think a man was right for the job. I was only being honest with the guy. I was speaking of all men in general
when I told him how inept a man would be at housekeeping, and I think he took it a little too personally."
Allowing a light mist to fall over her brushed-back
curls, Leslie smiled a determined smile and turned to
her attentive friend. "We both know it's true. Men can
be so inept in everything but sports. Actually, I'm just
waiting for him to make one real goof so I can convince
Mom to get rid of him. As I see it, his days as housekeeper here are limited."

"May I ask you a personal question?"

"Have I ever been able to stop you?" Leslie ban-
tered lightly, ready for the worst. To Carol, no topic was
off limits.

"When this man you claim you don't even like is

running around the house, why were you walking around upstairs dressed like that?"

"Carol!" Leslie sighed heavily.

"Hm?"

"You have too active an imagination. I'm just not used to having a man around—after all, it's been years. I simply forgot he was even in the house."

"You forgot." Carol sounded doubtful.

"Yes, I forgot. My mind was on the fact that I was late and needed to hurry."

Carol stared into space a moment, as if lost in thoughts of her own. Her blue eyes seemed to be looking right through Leslie, and there was a slight smile on her lips. Leslie, knowing immediately that her friend was lost in another one of her amazing daydreams, felt a twinge of something she could not exactly describe. Then it occurred to her that it was Randy Carol was probably thinking of—and that was what was causing her friend such obvious pleasure. She had been right; Carol certainly seemed quite impressed with Randy and his undeniable good looks. If she could only convince her friend that the male beauty he displayed ran only skin-deep. Inside he was a monster.

When Carol finally snapped out of her daze, she changed the subject abruptly, reminding Leslie that she was late. "Your guests are already beginning to arrive. I wasn't the first."

"I'm nearly ready," Leslie assured her as she applied a touch of perfume to her wrists and along her neck, just below each ear. Next she slipped into her dress of cinnamon gold, and adjusted its billowing sleeves, then secured its dark-brown sash at her waist. Taking one

last look in the mirror, she motioned for Carol to follow her out.

As the two walked the short distance to the main
stairway, Leslie noticed Randy's voice coming from the
guest bedroom. When she heard Lucille's voice reply
to whatever Randy had just said, she knew that the
man was at least doing what he had promised to do. He
was keeping Lucille busy so everything could be made
ready downstairs. Glancing down at her watch, Leslie
saw that it was five minutes to seven. Her mother had
planned to start the party at seven, and she was glad she
had managed to get ready on time after all. If she had
been late, she had a feeling Randy would have used it
against her in some manner, especially after the rude
way she had clearly expressed her views of tardiness to
him this morning.

"That housekeeper of your mom's may be bad news
to you, but he has got to have the sexiest voice ever
given man," Carol commented while they were de-
scending the stairs. She watched Leslie's reaction to her
words with a keen eye. When Leslie didn't reply, Carol
smiled and nodded to herself, as if her friend's obstinate silence had verified something for her. "Since you
don't care much for the man, you won't mind if I do a
little heavy flirting, will you?"

"No, go right ahead. It's your funeral." Leslie
shrugged, feeling everything inside of her tighten. For
what reason? She should have felt glad that Carol was
planning to keep him occupied. At least he wouldn't be
free to bother her. She would stand a better chance of
spending the evening in peace.

When they entered the dining room, they discovered

that everyone was already there. Knowing that Margaret had planned the small celebration to be a special surprise, everyone had entered without ringing or knocking at the front door. Most of them were neighbors, and knowing the house well, had come through the sliding glass door that opened to the back yard. They were trying their best to be quiet, but a low hum from all the excited whispering could be heard just outside the room.

The table was set, and Margaret was busy placing spoons into the many dishes warming on the buffet. A rich blend of appetizing aromas drifted through the room. The lights were low, and long tapered candles had been lit. At the head of the table was a bouquet of white roses and several of the smaller gifts and cards that had been brought. The huge package that held the new coat they had chosen for Lucille lay on a small table behind the place of honor. Everything seemed ready.

When Margaret noticed Leslie, she bustled over and whispered in an almost soundless voice for her to go back upstairs and tell Lucille that supper was ready. Margaret was almost giddy with anticipation. The tiny lines around her eyes and mouth deepened as she beamed with excitement.

Although it was not unusual for Carol to be around at dinnertime and Lucille had already seen her, Carol stayed behind. Knowing her lack of restraint, she was afraid she might be tempted to giggle or grin too much and cause Lucille to become suspicious.

When Leslie left the room, she could hear everyone being hushed behind her. She wondered if Lucille could possibly be unaware of all the clamor, quiet though it was, going on down there. At the top of the stairs, she saw Randy and Lucille busily inventorying the contents of the large linen closet. As she neared, she could hear Lucille explaining which sheets went on which beds and how often he would be expected to change them. Randy listened attentively.

"It's time for you two to call it quits," Leslie called out as she approached the pair. "Supper's ready, and Mom wants Lucille downstairs."

"I told your mother not to go to so much trouble." Lucille turned with the loving smile that had come to be so warmly familiar to Leslie. "It just seems absurd that she should be preparing my dinner after so many years of me being the one to do the meals."

Even though Lucille had openly protested Margaret's decision to cook this final supper, it was plain to see the woman was deeply touched. Leslie felt pleased that they could do this last special thing for her, but at the same time she ached with the knowledge that later tonight Lucille was leaving their lives, probably forever.

"Let's not keep her waiting," Leslie said cheerfully, reaching out for Lucille's hand. She tried not to react to the knowing wink and cockeyed grin Randy gave her behind Lucille's back. She looked away, hoping to ignore him entirely.

Lucille turned back to Randy, who was deadpan again, and offered to answer any more questions he might still have before going down to dinner. "I hate the thought of you having to stay any later than you already have. You certainly are to be complimented on your dedication to this new job. I'm just so glad that Margaret will have someone like you to replace me. I don't feel nearly as guilty about going now.''

Leslie was amazed at the sincerity in Randy's smile when he replied, ''I doubt I'll ever fully be able to replace you. You seem to be more than an employee around here. They seem to think of you as part of the family. As for more questions, I can't imagine any. We've already covered everything I can think of, and I do want to thank you for being so patient with me. You must be worn out from all the questions. I feel ashamed that I've monopolized so much of your time on your last afternoon to be with the Lovalls.''

''Nonsense. I was glad to do it.'' Lucille's gray eyes were sparkling with pride.

''You two had better hurry on downstairs before the food gets cold.'' Stepping between them, he nodded and continued to smile. ''I'll walk down with you so I can tell Mrs. Lovall good night before I leave.''

He was leaving now? Good. Leslie felt she would have a better chance of enjoying herself once he was gone—out of sight would mean out of mind. She could gladly do without his dominating presence this evening, or any evening for that matter.

Leading the way, Leslie listened as Lucille gave Randy still more last-minute pointers while they made their way down the stairs. But the closer they came to the dining room, the less attention she was able to pay to Lucille's chatter and the more aware she became of the silence in the room before them. She could barely stifle her own excitement as she considered what was about to happen. After taking a few steps into the can-

dlelit room and seeing everyone's eager faces staring at
the door, she, too, turned to watch Lucille's entry.

"Surprise!"

When the small group rushed to greet her, tears instantly filled Lucille's eyes, and her mouth fell open.
Little Joey Jackson was the first to reach her, and he
wrapped his small arms as far around Lucille's thick
waist as he could get them. The woman's hand automatically reached to smooth the child's curly black hair
as she smiled down into his sparkling green eyes. June
Langford, who was Joey's grandmother and Margaret's
next-door neighbor and best friend, leaned over the
boy to give Lucille a light embrace. At the same time,
Carol's mother, Beth Clifton, reached out and gave Lucille's arm a friendly squeeze.

As soon as Beth and Jane stepped back, Minnie Jef-
frey bounded forward and gave Lucille a generous hug,
mashing poor little Joey flat between them. Minnie was
Jane's long-time housekeeper, and as such had become
close friends with Lucille.

When Minnie finally released Lucille, giving Joey a
chance to refill his deflated lungs, Lucille turned to
Margaret, who had moved to stand beside Leslie, and
sobbed, "Why did you go and do this? I told you not to
go to any trouble and you went and did this."

"I couldn't help myself. I'm weak," Margaret replied with a slight shrug. With her own eyes glistening
with unshed tears, she asked in an emotionally choked
voice, "Why don't you quit your complaining and
come and open your presents?"

"Presents? For me? You shouldn't have!" Lucille's

eyes lit up like a small child's when she noticed the gaily wrapped packages at the far end of the table.

"You really think so?" Carol asked, stepping forward to examine the colorful gifts. Reaching for a small foil-wrapped box, she said teasingly, "Maybe I should take mine back then."

"Don't you dare!"

Everyone laughed and followed Lucille to the table. They wanted to watch her open the many presents, eager to see her reactions. While Lucille was busy tearing into the wrappings, Leslie was sure she heard the front door close. Glancing out into the entryway, she realized that Randy had left. Suddenly she felt disappointed that he'd done it so abruptly.

Returning her attention to Lucille, not wanting to dwell on newly awakened emotions that seemed linked to Randy, Leslie watched as she opened the gifts. With each one she opened, tears of gratitude and love filled Lucille's eyes, and she sobbed openly with happiness as she stood before the group wearing her new coat and clutching the other gifts, a delicately engraved silver music box, a deep-blue silk scarf, a tall brass bud vase, an electric foot massager, a small radio and a Fall Guy coloring book. She thanked her friends again and again for their generosity and told them just how she planned to put each gift to use. Joey was especially delighted to hear that Lucille intended to carry the coloring book—a gift from him and his dog Barky—right aboard the airplane so she wouldn't be bored during the long flight to Pennsylvania.

While Lucille carefully arranged her new possessions

on a long table near the hall door so everyone could view them at their leisure, the kitchen door swung open and in walked Randy, dressed handsomely in a dark-blue three-piece suit. His entrance was so unexpected that Leslie gasped aloud, and her hand went automatically to her mouth.

"Surely I'm not that frightening," he commented, glancing down with a raised brow as if trying to determine why she had reacted that way.

Carol took it upon herself to reply. "Not as far as I can tell." Then, looking heavenward, she added boldly, "If this man can be considered frightening in any way, please, Lord, let me die of fright."

Everyone laughed except Leslie. Randy accepted the remark as a compliment and thanked Carol with a slight bow. "I appreciate such words from a lady as lovely as yourself."

Although not impressed with the conversation, Leslie was, however, amazed at the quick change Randy had made, and when he came farther into the room, she noticed that he seemed just as comfortable in his suit as he had in jeans and a work shirt. She had not tried to envision him in a suit before. It had not even occurred to her that he might ever wear one. She was stunned by the effect the change in attire had on him, making him elegantly handsome in contrast to the rugged good looks he'd displayed earlier. And it was impossible not to notice how the dark blue of his suit made his crystal eyes appear even clearer by comparison. Leslie wondered how many women had become lost in the shining depths of those uncanny eyes.

"Ladies, if you will be seated, I would like to begin

serving." He offered them one of his most charming smiles, and Leslie became aware that every female eye in the room was staring approvingly at him—especially Carol's.

"I see we do have one gentleman among us," he amended quickly, having glanced down and noticed little Joey. "So, ladies and gentleman, if you would please be seated."

Leslie took her seat along with the rest, continuing to stare disbelievingly at Randy. How had he changed so quickly yet managed to look so fresh and perfect? His clothes were immaculate, his hair flawless. Leslie felt disgusted that it had taken her over an hour to get ready, with results that had not been nearly so grand.

Once everyone had taken their seats, Randy carried the dishes around, one at a time, until he had served everyone. Leslie had fully expected him to disappear after he had finished with the last dish, but instead he stood back in a corner and watched the group eat, coming forward with wine or water whenever he noticed a glass getting low. Knowing he was nearby, watching, made it hard for her to enjoy her meal. She was oddly nervous—but she noticed that Randy was not having a similar effect on Carol. In fact, Carol seemed to have quite a thirst tonight, and Randy had to make numerous trips to her side to refill her wine glass. Leslie also noticed that Carol was not giving her food the same attention as she was giving her wineglass and had no doubt her friend was going to be rather tipsy by the end of the meal.

"Carol, what do you think of this chicken Kiev?" she asked quietly, gently elbowing her friend in order

to get her attention. She hoped the question would encourage Carol at least to try enough of the food to be
able to form an opinion.

"The Kiev is wonderful," Carol whispered back,
then, with an impish grin, she added in an even lower
voice, "So's the service."

As she spoke, Randy was coming around the table
with a freshly opened bottle of wine. Although Leslie
had not touched her wineglass, preferring water to wine
with her meal, Randy paused and poured a bit more of
the red liquid into it, letting his arm brush up against
hers with obvious intent. She was certain his action had
been deliberate, yet she didn't make an effort to pull
away. Although she had found the brief contact infuri-
ating, she tried to convince herself that she was allowing him to get away with the obvious because she
preferred not to make a scene in front of the guests.
She refused to consider the fact that she had actually
enjoyed his touch, and promised herself the pleasure of
a full reprimand for his forward behavior later, in private. He would not get off too lightly, either.

Leslie smiled as she thought of their next little con-
frontation, but her smile soon faded when she became
aware of how quickly he had moved on to fill Carol's
glass. She found it oddly discomfiting that Carol was
turning on her sweet Southern charm and Randy
seemed to be thoroughly enjoying it. When Carol had
mentioned flirting heavily with Randy this evening,
Leslie now felt, her friend had grossly understated her
intentions. Carol was giving him a full dose, being as
sexy as she knew how. No man stood a chance when
Carol turned on her sultry charm, and Leslie was, as

always, amazed at how well it seemed to work for Carol, knowing that such behavior on her part would have only served to make her feel foolish.

Never really having experienced jealousy before, Leslie tried to ignore the icy turmoil growing in her. When she could no longer deny that something painful was happening to her, and getting worse with each word the two of them exchanged, she quickly decided to label the raw, awful ache she felt as concern for her friend. Carol did not know what sort of buffoon she was getting tangled up with. Leslie did.

Trying to pull Carol's attention away from Randy, who had remained at her friend's side a little longer than necessary, Leslie nudged Carol with her elbow again. When Carol turned in response, Leslie paused, searching for something to say. Finally she said, foolishly, inanely, "Don't eat too much, Carol. You need to save room for the dessert."

That seemed especially dumb, knowing that Carol had barely touched her food at all—anyone glancing down at her plate should have been able to realize that.

Lifting her wineglass and taking another sip, Carol smiled gaily. "Oh, don't worry, I still have plenty of room for dessert. What are we having? Something special?"

"Cake."

"Just cake?" Carol looked at her friend as if she were a bit teched. She could have cake any day. "The way you were telling me to be sure and save room, I thought we were in for a real treat."

Knowing she had to save face before Carol put too much into her reason for having spoken up at all, Leslie quickly added, "It's a cake we had made wishing Lucille good luck. You wouldn't want to insult her by having to refuse a piece because you were too full. She might be offended."

"Wouldn't want that," Carol commented, raising an eyebrow while she carefully studied Leslie's face for further signs of idiocy. After a moment, she laughed a short, delighted laugh and took another long drink of her wine. Now it was Leslie's turn to look at Carol as if she might be a bit teched.

"Speaking of the cake, I think it's about time I brought it in. It seems most of the guests are nearly finished." Randy excused himself with a polite nod to the two of them; but before turning to leave, he winked down at Carol and set the half-filled bottle beside her. He added, chuckling, "Maybe I'd better leave this here. You may have to serve yourself while I'm gone."

"You're very considerate," Carol drawled up at him, accepting the bottle with a smile. Then, turning back to Leslie, she bit her lower lip and stated bluntly, "That man's gorgeous. I'll bet he's super in bed."

Never shocked by Carol's blatant remarks anymore, Leslie argued, "Looks can be deceiving."

"I know. You've already told me you don't particularly care for the man. We obviously have different opinions about him, but then, when have we ever totally agreed on anything?" Carol shrugged playfully. Then, smiling a wicked, she-devil smile, she leaned toward Leslie and added, "You may think he's a bad guy, but I don't. On the contrary, I'll bet he's very, very good, and if things go right this evening, I'll be able to let you know which of us is right about him, maybe even by morning."

For no reason that she could see, Leslie felt wounded, as though something had torn right through her body and soul. She had never been this concerned over Carol's affairs before; why was she so upset now? For the first time, it fully occurred to her that she could be jealous. But why? Was it because Carol seemed to be able to get along with Randy so well when she herself couldn't hold a civil conversation with the man? Certainly it was not because she cared for Randy herself. She knew for a fact that she detested him. In fact, she wanted him out of the house and out of her life. No, she reasoned adamantly, she wasn't feeling jealousy. But what was she feeling?

Before she could dwell on it any longer, Randy came in with the cake and placed it in front of Lucille. And after another teary protest from the guest of honor, the cake was cut and served.

At the end of the meal, the ladies retired to the parlor with their coffee, leaving Joey to gorge himself on a second ample piece of cake. Being occupied with conversation for the rest of the evening, Leslie did not have time to ponder the inner ache that was now gnawing at her constantly.

Shortly after nine, Beth Clifton approached Leslie, wanting to know if she had seen Carol. "We came together, and since we're in my car tonight, I'm supposed to see her home. I haven't been feeling well and I'm ready to leave, but I don't know where my darling daughter is."

"Actually, I haven't seen her in quite a while," Leslie admitted as she glanced around the room. "But I'll help you look for her."

Feeling oddly disturbed, she excused herself politely from the small group and walked out with Beth in search of Carol. She had a sinking feeling she would find Carol in the kitchen, where Randy was supposed to be cleaning up, and just before they reached the kitchen door, she knew she had guessed right. Carol's laughter came drifting out to meet them.

"Sounds as if Carol's had a bit much to drink," Beth commented, looking slightly embarrassed as another outburst of laughter reached them.

"A bit," Leslie commented dryly. Then, forcing a cheerfulness she did not feel, she added, "But then, when have you ever known Carol to refuse a good glass of wine?"

Steeling herself against what they might see, Leslie stepped ahead of Beth and entered the kitchen first. She couldn't have been more surprised if she'd found them dancing on the ceiling covered with whipped cream. Randy had removed his jacket and rolled up his shirt sleeves. His muscular arms were plunged elbow-deep in dishwater. Carol was standing right beside him with a huge dish towel, slowly drying the pieces as he handed them to her.

"What's going on here?" Beth was first to speak. "How did you ever manage to get Carol to help like that?"

"I have certain powers," Randy answered in a low, ominous tone. "She came in here to see if there was any more chilled wine, and I simply willed her with my mind to stay and dry these dishes for me. Sometimes I scare myself with my uncanny powers."

"Do me a favor," Beth injected with a wry smile. "Will her to do her own laundry and to quit bringing it over to my house by the carloads."

Leslie grew impatient with what she felt was a silly conversation. "Just why are you two washing the dishes by hand? Mom does have a dishwasher, you know. It's that thing next to the sink with all the buttons on it. You do know how to work a dishwasher, don't you? Or are you just out for a little overtime?" Her voice had sounded sharper than she had intended. She realized that silence had grown heavy in the room.

"The dishwasher is full, and rather than leave your mother with a mess to face when all the guests leave, I decided to go ahead and wash these last few items by hand. And to set the record straight, I'm not claiming any overtime. It was my idea to work tonight."

Leslie did not know how to respond to that. Luckily Beth prevented her from having to reply at all by asking Carol if she was ready to leave.

"Not really." Carol frowned, glancing down at her watch. "It's only nine-fifteen—why are you in such a hurry to leave?"

"I'm tired, and my head is beginning to hurt. I'm sorry to make you leave so early, but I really am not feeling well. I don't think I'm fully over the flu yet."

"Oh, all right," Carol said, clearly not ready to go. Then, as if a wonderful idea had suddenly presented itself, she smiled brightly and turned to Leslie. "Why don't I just ride back over to the apartment with you? Then I can stay a while longer."

"I'd be glad to take you home, but I promised to drive Lucille out to the airport at eleven. She's catching a late flight out tonight. It will probably be close to one before I get home."

"I thought she wasn't leaving until tomorrow."

"She found out there was a flight out tonight that would take her directly there, and she would be able to arrive in time to be at the hospital when her daughter is released tomorrow. I'll be glad to let you ride with me, but I warn you, I won't be getting home until way after midnight."

"Tell you what," Randy broke in. "Since your mother does want to leave now and you would rather stay a while longer, why don't you just let me take you home? It will be another hour before I'm ready to go. You would be able to visit that much longer."

"That would certainly help solve the problem," Carol said with an appreciative nod, her eyes widening with anticipation. "Thank you."

Actually, Leslie thought it was a terrible solution to the problem, but she managed not to say so out loud. The best solution would have been for Carol to go on with her mother now—that would have parted these two before something regrettable developed. The thought of Carol and Randy leaving together made her feel ill. Carol was too much of a free spirit. Although many times Leslie had admired her for it, right now her friend's reckless, easygoing manner worried her. Carol had made her intentions where Randy was concerned very clear, and the thought of that made Leslie want to cry out in frustrated anger. Poor Carol didn't even know what she was getting herself into.

Chapter Four

Leslie hadn't felt so depressed since right after her father had died and she had realized that the responsibility of Lovall's was falling on her shoulders. It had taken her months to pull herself out of that melancholy mood. As she drove back to her apartment, she wondered how long the overwhelming misery she now felt would last. The gloomy mood had started even before Carol and Randy had left her mother's house together, although it had grown steadily worse since then. The final straw had been having to say good-bye to Lucille at the airport, knowing there was little hope of seeing her again anytime soon. She had tried to fight back the tears but had lost.

She still had the urge to cry even as she pulled into the entrance of the Willow Wood Apartments, named after the huge, draping trees that graced the enormous complex. Pressing her lips into a fine line, Leslie was determined to get her emotions back under control. When would she ever learn that crying never solved anything? Crying was a sign of weakness, and she had been taught by her father to overcome her weaknesses. He had allowed her mother to cry, but never her.

"Someone must be having a party," she mumbled to herself when she realized that there were no vacant parking spaces near her apartment. As she drove along the darkened drive, she began to look for an empty place to park. It seemed absurd that she might have to park in the visitors' lot and walk back half a block, when it was probably visitors who were claiming all those other spots. As she searched for a place for her car, she couldn't help but notice a certain red Chevy coupe parked right beside Carol's silver Buick Regal.

Glancing immediately up at Carol's apartment on the second floor, she noticed that the light was on. Randy was still up there in her apartment. What could they be doing up there at this hour? No, she did not want to think about that. If he had decided to do more than take her home, that was none of her business. Why should she give it a second thought?

Finally locating a parking spot, Leslie walked quickly to her apartment, trying not to glance toward Carol's apartment or at the bright-red roadster. She realized she was a little shaky as she tried to fit the key into her lock, and decided it was not entirely because of Randy and Carol but from a combination of things, including the fact that it was cold and she had just watched Lucille board the airplane. Even though she was concerned for her friend, there was nothing she could do about it now. She was not Carol's keeper.

Taking a hot shower, Leslie quickly got ready for bed. The sooner she could get to sleep and forget all the things that seemed to be making her so unhappy the better. Hugging a pillow to her, she found sleep amazingly obtainable, so much so that she jumped with a start when a heavy pounding on her door awoke her an hour later.

"Coming," she called out, blinking with confusion. Glancing at the digital clock on the nightstand near her bed, she wondered who would be knocking at two in the morning. Her first thought was that there had been an emergency of some sort, and she felt a lump form in her throat as she made her way through the dark to the door.

"Who is it?" she asked as she neared the door.

"It's Carol" came the reply in a loud, raspy whisper. "Let me in. It's freezing out here!"

Leslie let out an exasperated breath. What did Carol want? Did she intend to give her the rundown on her romantic evening? If that was so, Leslie wasn't sure she wanted to hear it, but knowing how persistent Carol could be, she reached for the light, then opened the door and let her friend in.

"You won't believe it. You simply won't believe it!" Carol was bubbling with excitement as she rushed into the room. A short blast of cold air followed her inside.

"Carol, do you know what time it is?"

Glancing down at her watch, Carol replied, "Yes, it's just after two, why?"

"Just curious," Leslie mumbled, realizing Carol had not taken the hint. "Did Randy finally leave?"

"A few minutes ago, and wait until you hear!" Carol said excitedly. Her azure eyes sparkled with delight, and Leslie cowered at the thought of having to listen to all the details she knew Carol would not leave out. She had heard play-by-play accounts of Carol's evenings before and there were no details her friend would not share with her.

Curling up with her bare feet beneath her on one end of the Victorian couch, she watched as Carol flitted about the room, unable to contain her excitement. "So, Carol, how'd it go?"

"Not exactly the way I'd thought. Wait until you hear!"

Leslie felt she had waited long enough, realizing that if she had to wait any longer she was going to throttle her best friend. Having resigned herself to having to hear it all, she was ready to get it over. "So tell me already."

"The guy is wild about you!" Carol gasped out, her eyes sparkling.

"They always are," Leslie replied, having misunderstood what her friend had said. "You've always affected men that way."

"Not me, *you*. All the man could do was ask questions about you. We just spent three hours up in my apartment and most of that time we talked about you. And do you know what he came right out and told me?"

"What?" Raising a brow in disbelief, Leslie leaned forward. She was rapidly growing more interested in this conversation, even though she wasn't sure she believed any of it.

"He said that he intends to have you." Carol's eyes looked as if they were going to explode. "One way or another, the man intends to seduce you. He's simply wild about you."

"Aren't you exaggerating a little?"

"I don't think so. All he wanted to do was learn all he could about you. He clearly was not interested in me. And he did actually come right out and tell me that he intended to have you. He admitted that you might not be willing just yet, but that in time he would have you right where he wanted you."

"And did you ever stop to think that he could mean something else by that? Where he wants me might be under his thumb. Remember, I told you how he might be seeking revenge for what I said to him and how rudely I treated him when we first met. He may have been seeking facts about me in order to find my vulnerable spots. The man is pretty cagey. I seriously doubt he's romantically inclined."

"Oh, yes he is," Carol insisted. "You should have seen him when I told him about John LaFerney. He tensed up and wanted to know more about your relationship with him."

"And you told him?"

Carol, wincing at the mortified sound in Leslie's voice, admitted, "I guess I did tell him a little about it."

"What? What did you tell him?"

"That you two seemed to have sort of an understanding. He wanted to know if it was serious between you, and I had to be honest. I told him I didn't think so, but that I really was not sure. I didn't want to spoil your chances with him. After all, he's crazy about you."

"Oh, he's crazy, all right—he should be declared legally insane. And if you think I'm going to let myself get involved with an impudent, disrespectful, self-centered creature like that, you must be crazy, too. Besides, I'm not easily fooled. The man has something sinister up his sleeve, and I'm not about to fall for it. I just hope you didn't give him any information he can use against me."

"Why can't you believe that he actually is attracted to you?" Plopping down on the opposite end of the couch, Carol sighed in exasperation. "After all, you are not exactly dead meat. You're very attractive. You dress well and *usually* have a great head on your shoulders."

Leslie noticed the emphasis Carol had placed on the word "usually" and lifted her eyebrows, nonplussed. "I can tell by the way we react to each other that he isn't interested in the way I think. There's bad chemistry between us. If he is interested in anything, it's how to even the score."

"Just suppose I was right. Just suppose he really is attracted to you and indeed hopes to win you over. Aren't you in any way attracted to him?"

"No."

"Not even a little?"

"Look, I'll admit the man is nice-looking."

"And has a body that won't quit," Carol commented with a wicked grin.

"I'll agree, he's in good shape," Leslie conceded. "But even though he isn't bad to look at, he is also the most aggravating person I've ever had the misfortune to meet. And if you were hoping to play some sort of matchmaker, forget it. I'd much rather have someone dependable and reliable like John."

"You mean someone *safe* like John, don't you?"

Boy, that sounded awfully close to the truth, but so what? Why should she risk getting more involved than she cared to? With John she had companionship without any emotional strings. They had a lot in common and did not have to strain their relationship by getting too serious. Not wanting ever to become dependent on any man, especially after seeing what such a weakness had done to her mother, she felt that John was the perfect man for her. When her father had died, Leslie found out that not only had her mother's entire existence been tied into him, hers had been, too. She had never felt so lost than when her father died. She had grown dependent on him for making decisions for her as well. Never again.

"And what's wrong with that, Carol?"

"I wish I could make you see just what *is* wrong with that. I wish just once you would fall in love and find out how great romance can be."

"Let's not get into that again. It's just another one of those things we will never agree on. I will not end up like my mother did. I will not allow another man to destroy my identity even in the name of romance. It's not worth the price a woman has to pay."

Carol crossed her arms and leaned back into the corner of the couch. She stared at her friend in defeat. Narrowing her eyes, she said quietly, "One of these days, Leslie, you are going to find out just how great love can be. It's not something you should be so afraid of."

"Car-ol..."

"Okay, okay. I just wanted to tell you what Randy had said. I thought you might like to know. And I might add that I hope he's right. I happen to be on his side.''

"I appreciate your loyalty," Leslie retorted tonelessly. Her lips formed a tight, flat line. "But I still think you have the wrong idea. The only thing he wants is to come out on top."

"That's one way to put it."

"Carol!"

"Sorry, I couldn't resist it."

Grinning in spite of her annoyance with her friend, Leslie went on to explain. "What I was trying to say is that he's interested only in putting me down. As I told you, he didn't take too kindly to some of my remarks. But there's no use in us arguing about whatever his intentions are. Time will tell."

"Speaking of time, I need my beauty sleep." Carol yawned. Her excitement had subsided, and now she appeared a little droopy-eyed. "We can talk more about this later. No matter which of us is right about Randy, it will be interesting to see the outcome."

Moments later, Carol bade her final farewell and Leslie crawled back into bed with new things to think about. She was worried about what Randy might have planned for her. She honestly did not believe he was interested in her romantically. Even so, she had to admit the thought was in some way stimulating, because every time she allowed herself to wonder about the idea, preposterous as it seemed, she felt her pulse quicken. She also had to admit to herself that she was selfishly relieved that nothing had happened between Randy and Carol.

The next morning Leslie was amazed at how good

she felt for someone who had only gotten a few hours of sleep. Even though her sleep had been limited, it had done wonders. She no longer felt that heavy depression that had overtaken her the evening before. Quickly, she got dressed and hurried over to her mother's house for breakfast. It occurred to her that she was more eager than usual to get over there, and her only answer to that was her interest in seeing how he planned to get even. She found this undeclared feud of theirs to be rather challenging. He had a lot of rethinking to do if he thought he was going to get the best of her. She was more determined than ever to see his ridiculous job taken away from him.

"Good morning, Ms. Lovall." Randy greeted her with one of those endearing smiles that Leslie had learned to be wary of.

"Good morning," she responded, with a pert smile of her own.

"We thought you were going to be late," he said meaningfully. "Your mother is already in the dining room waiting for you. Breakfast is ready when you are."

"Then bring it on. I'm famished." Tossing her coat at him, she walked past him toward the dining room.

Although the meal passed uneventfully, Leslie was aware of how carefully Randy seemed to be watching her. She felt certain he was plotting something fiendish against her, but she found the thought of that invigorating. She could hardly contain her own evil smile when she thought of how surprised he would be when his little game of cat and mouse ended with the cat out in the cold and the mouse still in charge of the house.

She had not realized that she had been staring at him until he approached her moments after her mother had left the room to finish getting ready for work.

"Is there something about me you don't like—that is, besides the fact that I'm a man?" he asked casually, beginning to clear the table. "Is there a particular reason you've been staring daggers through me?"

Stunned by his directness, Leslie was unable to find an adequate answer for the instant antagonism she had felt for him. "You certainly have an active imagination. I've hardly noticed you." She could almost feel her nose grow with that lie.

"Maybe it's just my imagination, then, but I could swear you've been staring holes right through me. I don't know why, but I get the feeling you don't care to have me around, that my presence bothers you in some way. Maybe it's the toothpaste I use, or maybe I ate the wrong kind of cereal for breakfast?"

Leslie found herself smiling at the absurdity. The man had a definite short in his main circuit. "Why don't we just chalk it up to bad chemistry between us?"

Pulling out the chair next to her, he sat down beside her, smiling suggestively as he leaned toward her. "Oh, there's plenty of chemistry between us all right, but not all of it is bad."

"Mr. Brinnad!"

"Could you please call me something besides Mr. Brinnad? That makes me feel older than I care to feel. And I'm also tired of calling you Ms. Lovall."

"Well, I must admit there are things I'd rather call you," she began with a menacing look in her dark eyes. "But I think you'd prefer me to call you Mr. Brinnad."

"I'd prefer you call me Randy," he replied with an amused chuckle. "And I know what I'd like to call you."

She knew better than to ask, but for the life of her she couldn't stop herself. "And just what would that be?"

"Mine," he said simply, winking at her in a most provocative manner before reaching for the stack of dirty dishes he had gathered and rising to leave. "But until I am able to call you mine, I will settle for calling you Leslie."

The man was incorrigible. "You will continue to call me Ms. Lovall," she shouted to his back as he disappeared through the kitchen door.

"No, I won't," he shouted back over his shoulder.

"Mother!" she found herself calling out childishly. Why this sudden urge to tell on him? She was appalled at her own reaction. She hadn't been prone to tattling since she was in the first grade. What good would it do, anyway?

"What is it?" She heard her mother's voice coming from the stairway.

Taking a deep breath to calm herself, she responded in a barely controlled voice, "Are you ready to go?"

"Just need to get my coat" came her mother's cheery reply. She waited in the hall doorway until Leslie had joined her, and the two made their way to the entrance.

Randy appeared from out of nowhere with their coats and first helped Margaret on with hers, then held Leslie's open for her to slip into. Reluctantly, Leslie turned her back to him and eased her arms into the armholes. When she felt the coat being lifted onto her shoulders, she was aware of his warm hands lingering against the sensitive skin along her neck. Jerking away from him, she thanked him curtly and stepped away.

"My pleasure." He smiled, his dimples taking over his lean cheeks.

She could imagine that it had indeed been his pleasure. He had gotten the reaction he was probably hoping for. She wished she had been able to simply ignore it.

"See you at lunch," Margaret called as she stepped out into the cold, pulling her collar up as she went.

"I'll have it ready at one," he assured them. "One is all right with you, isn't it, Leslie?"

Aware of the emphasis he'd placed on her first name, she glared at him before following her mother outside. She walked briskly toward her car, purposely leaving the door for him to close and he took advantage of the open door to watch her march off to her car.

How he loved that temper of hers, he mused.

As the morning progressed, Leslie's thoughts kept returning to Randy. Just the thought of him and the way he insisted on going against her made her blood boil. She hoped fervently he was finding that with Lucille gone the work was more than he'd anticipated. She hoped he was struggling helplessly with his duties, falling further and further behind. When they returned for lunch, she wanted to find him busy wrestling with the laundry while their meal burned slowing on the stove. Then she could point to him self-righteously and tell her mother that she had told her so. It was no job for a man, much less an egotistical barbarian like

Randy Brinnad. Just the thought of his probable predicament brought a smile to her face.

Because a brisk wind now accompanied the cold December temperatures, Leslie parked in the garage when they returned home, and they took the short, enclosed walkway to the kitchen. As they neared, Leslie was eager to find Randy in harried confusion, but when she heard his beautiful golden voice singing happy Christmas carols just inside the kitchen door, she had a feeling she was about to be disappointed. Sure enough, when they stepped into the warmth of the room, he greeted them cheerfully with a long wooden spoon poised in his hand.

"Good afternoon," he chimed gaily. He seemed ridiculously at home in the kitchen. Only Margaret returned his greeting.

To Leslie's dismay, the room was immaculate. There were no dirty dishes stacked in the sink or lying on the counters. Everything was in order. Several pots were on the stove, steaming slightly, and a tray containing serving bowls sat nearby waiting for use.

"I just put the rolls in. Lunch will be ready to serve by the time you've washed up and are seated." he said offhandedly, then turned his attention back to the stove. "The table has been set."

Unable to believe that he was able to cope with his duties this well, Leslie did not follow her mother upstairs. Instead, she walked purposefully down the back hallway to the laundry room and glanced in, ready to comment on the fact that Lucille usually had the laundry finished before lunch. The dirty clothes hamper had been overflowing last night when she had brought in the soiled tablecloth, but now it was closed and looked suspiciously empty. There were no clothes to be seen at all, and no sign of the tablecloth, either.

Stepping inside, she lifted the top of the hamper. It *was* empty. Next she lifted the lid on the washing machine. It was empty, too. So was the dryer. Where was all that dirty laundry? She was just about to check to see if it had been stuffed into the supply closet when Randy's deep voice startled her.

"You're not going to find it in there. I've already finished the laundry and put everything away. Sorry to disappoint you."

Leslie's first thought was to deny that he had guessed what her mission had been, but she couldn't come up with another plausible excuse for being there. Rather than give him the satisfaction of admitting anything, she simply brushed past him, ignoring his amused grin, and went upstairs. It took several minutes of seething and angry pacing about her former room before she could come downstairs again.

Lunch was regrettably delicious. Margaret complimented him over and over, while Leslie only offered a begrudging nod or two. She was not at all happy about the outcome of all this. Her trip upstairs had proved that he'd already straightened up there as well. She'd found that the bathroom she'd left in a mess the evening before was now sparkling clean. There was something fishy about it all. She was still not ready to believe that he was as competent as it appeared.

When time came for her to go back to work, he had already washed the lunch dishes and was busy getting the vacuum out. Again he was humming a light and lively Christmas carol as if he didn't have a care in the world.

Randy truly did enjoy his work. He found considerable pleasure in knowing he was doing something constructive with his time, that his efforts would be evident at the end of the day, unlike desk work. Housekeeping was almost a form of art for him. To look over a sparkling clean house at the end of the day, knowing he was the one responsible for how wonderful it looked, had rewards parallel to none. And he found this job particularly rewarding in that every time he did a really terrific job, it seemed to drive Leslie Lovall completely bonkers.

The next couple of days followed a similar pattern. Every time Leslie stopped by, whether for breakfast or lunch or an evening visit, Randy had the housework well in hand. Not only was the house just as spotless as when Lucille had been there, but little things like dripping faucets and squeaky hinges had been taken care of as well. It bothered Leslie no end that he was so talented. Late evenings, which would be after he had left at four-thirty, she would peek into pantries and closets and be frustrated to discover everything in its place. When was he going to bungle something? Surely he couldn't keep this up.

The worst of it was his cheerful mood. The more cheerful he acted, the more disgruntled she became. At least she only had to put up with his company in the mornings and during lunch. He was usually gone by the time she came by in the evenings, so it surprised her when she pulled into the driveway late Friday evening and discovered his car still there. What surprised her even more was the scene that greeted her when she stepped into the front room.

"Leslie, isn't it beautiful?" Margaret exclaimed when she noticed her daughter standing in the doorway. She was busy handing small ornaments up to Randy, who was standing at the top of a stepladder and placing them on the tree. The lights had already been strung and twinkled brightly. Christmas music was playing on the radio to help round out the holiday scene.

"Yes, it is," she admitted. It was one of the largest, most lovely Christmas trees she'd ever seen. It was so tall that a few inches would have to be cut off the top to keep it from bending at the ceiling.

"Come help us decorate," Margaret said gaily, her face radiating Christmas spirit.

Leslie stood in wonder of the moment. There had not been a Christmas tree in the house since her father's death. Even the year before, when she had finally resumed having holiday gatherings, her mother had never gotten into the mood to decorate, other than to put the traditional wreath on the front door. Looking around, Leslie noticed the fireplace draped in holly and bright red bows. There were fat red candles on tall brass stands all along the mantle. Many of the tables were appointed with thick pots of red or white poinsettias, and a ceramic Santa smiled from his position on the hearth. Leslie couldn't imagine what had brought all this on. Whatever had happened, she couldn't help but blink back tears of joy.

"What do you want me to do?" she asked, more than willing to help.

"Start putting ornaments on the lower branches while Randy puts on the ones up there," Margaret said, nodding at the dusty boxes that had been stored away for so long.

The next hour was spent singing along with the holiday music on the radio and laughing over memories of Christmases past. Leslie was so glad that her mother no longer found the memories depressing, as she had in the past. They were even able to discuss her father directly without the mood becoming morbid or sad.

"You know, I don't know why Dad even bothered asking me what I wanted for Christmas," Leslie remembered. "No matter what I told him, he always went out and bought whatever struck his fancy at the moment."

"The reason he sometimes didn't get you what you asked for is because you asked for things like a football or a set of drums. Not exactly what a father would want his beautiful young daughter to have. He was set on making a lady out of you."

"Well, I'd much rather have had a football than tea sets or baby dolls. Why couldn't he wait to make a lady out of me later on, when I'd finally figured out I was a girl? You just don't know how badly I wanted a real professional football all those years I asked for one."

"I can't imagine you having a problem figuring out you were a girl," Randy commented thoughtfully. "I figured that out the instant I met you. And as I recall, you were pretty quick to notice I was a man."

Leslie raised an eyebrow at that remark, but she was in too good a mood to let it bother her. "Carol and I were the only two girls in a neighborhood full of boys, so we grew up playing things like Army, football, Man from U.N.C.L.E. and baseball. It never occurred to us to play house or dolls. You don't know how mad I got when I turned fourteen and Dad laid down those new laws—"No more tackle football." He also forbade me to call any boys on the phone after that, just because I was a girl and a girl had her place. I couldn't believe what a raw deal it was to be a girl until later on when I started dating and found out it was the guys that paid for everything—or at least that was the way it was back then."

"But your father finally convinced you that you were a girl?" Randy asked with a chuckle, glad her father had somehow succeeded.

"Yes, and I took it like a man." Leslie laughed. "But I've never quite gotten over the disappointment of never having received a football for Christmas. I was such a deprived child."

"My heart bleeds," Randy said, wiping imaginary tears from his eyes, and they all laughed.

It wasn't until the tree was completely finished and they were standing back admiring their handiwork that Margaret realized she was hungry. While Randy and Leslie worked together to clean up the empty boxes and the ornaments that had gotten broken, Margaret went to check on the rich Texas stew that Randy had left on the stove to simmer.

For once Leslie was not irritated by Randy's cheerful mood—in fact, she shared in it. They continued talking about Christmas-related things as they carried the containers back to the attic. When they returned for the last load, there was just enough for one person to have to make the final trip. Being the first one into the room, Leslie bent over, gathered up the last few boxes, and hauled them away. Upon returning, she found Randy standing just inside the door with one of those grins on his face.

Stepping into the doorway, she gave him a suspiciously inquiring look, and he answered by simply pointing to the doorframe overhead. Mistletoe! Someone, and she had a pretty good idea who, had tacked a small sprig of mistletoe to the doorframe right over where she was standing. She stared up at it in disbelief.

When she looked back down to tell him to forget it, she discovered he'd already made his move. His lips were on hers before she was able to voice her protest. A strange warmth flooded her senses, making her feel a bit lightheaded, but she wasn't about to give in to it. She brought her hands up to his chest in order to push him away. The effort only made him tighten his hold, pulling her closer in the process. The more she struggled, the more demanding the kiss grew. Finally, Leslie decided to simply let him have his kiss and get it over with.

She had not expected the kiss to affect her very much anyway. Kissing never had. But this kiss was somehow different, and when her hands moved up to his neck of their own volition, she knew she was in trouble. She felt an unfamiliar hunger, an awakening of sorts inside her. A warm tide surged through her, urging her on, lessening her desire to escape. Although her mind warned her she should make another effort to free herself, her body willed her to press closer to explore the pleasure she was finding in the kiss.

Mysteriously, the kiss sent her deep into a turbulent sea of emotions, many of them totally new, others vaguely familiar. When his hands began to move down her spine until they came to rest on the softness of her hips, fire coursed through her veins, sending its sensual heat to every fiber of her being. The pleasure of his touch was drugging her senses. She knew that if she didn't act now to save herself from being overtaken completely by these emotions, she would be lost to them. Leslie allowed herself to savor one last moment before finally letting her common sense win out and pulling quickly away.

Stepping back, she found herself gasping for air. Everything inside her was still reeling, and she was keenly aware that it was because of the kiss. Never had a kiss done that to her. She found it hard to believe that the simple touching of lips could set fire to her very soul. And it occurred to her that it could very easily become habit-forming.

"That had to be the most arousing kiss I've ever experienced," Randy commented gruffly, still struggling with his own breath. "I had a feeling it would be good, but never did I dream it would be that good."

Leslie did not know how to respond to that.

"Remind me to get more mistletoe. I want to cover this place in it."

Leslie still did not know how to respond. She decided she must be in shock. She had never been at a total loss for words before.

"Oh, my, you've stepped back under the mistletoe," he commented, with a lift of his brow. "You know what that means."

"No!" The word seemed to come out of nowhere. Stepping away from him even farther, she tried quickly to sort out her feelings. None of this made sense. Here she had been kissed by a man she could barely tolerate and she had practically dissolved in his arms. It was not the right reaction at all. This needed to be reasoned out.

"Yes," came his reply, and he moved closer.

"No."

"Oh, yes."

"Randy, I said no."

"Randy said yes."

"Oh, Randy," she sighed as once again his lips descended on hers with a maddening intensity. Again her senses fell prey to the lunacy of passion. Her self-control had been taken out of her hands and put into the hands of a madman. Her mind could see that she could be becoming this man's pawn, but her heart just didn't seem to care. All that seemed to matter at this moment was kissing Randy. She wanted to feast on the sensations that invaded her body.

As the kiss deepened, he pulled her body tight against his, and she felt the heat from him radiating right through her winter clothing. Suddenly, his hands were beneath her knit blouse, searching. An alarm went off inside her, but she chose to ignore it. Timidly, she eased her hands up and down his back, marveling in the feel of his firm muscles, while his fingers worked their magic on the sensitive skin along her ribs and his thumbs played witht the lacy edge of her bra.

Curiosity, mixed with newly developing desire, quietly spurred her on, and she slid her hands beneath his heavy sweater and allowed herself the pleasure of running her fingertips over his warm, naked skin. She gasped when his thumbs slipped beneath the soft fabric covering her breasts and came into contact with the swelling peaks. Again the silent alarm went off, and this time she paid attention. She pulled away.

"Randy, no, we can't."

"You're right. Not here, anyway."

"You don't understand. I don't want to get involved like this. Not with you or anyone."

"So? I do."

"So, we can't be doing this. It can only lead to heaven knows where."

"Oh, I know where it can lead," he assured her, narrowing his eyes as if trying to transmit a thought to her.

"Randy, I don't want to get intimate with anyone. I don't want to be committed to anyone. Don't you understand that it would put strings on me that I don't want? I can't stand the thought of being emotionally bound to anyone. It only leads to trouble and heartache. I'm fiercely independent, and I don't want to chance losing my identity to any man. I can't stand to see women so helpless and wimpy that they can't make their own decisions because they've let men take over. They can't even lead their own lives."

"It doesn't have to be like that," he told her. His brows dipped with concern. He realized she was dead serious about what she was saying, and that worried him.

"It's always like that. My own mother was like that. When my father died, she couldn't even cope with daily life. She was so dependent on Dad that it took a long time before she could function as a person on her own. Only recently has she resumed living anything near a normal life. It was awful."

"It doesn't have to be like that," he repeated, wondering how he was going to make her see how one-dimensional her view of love was.

"Whenever anyone tries to get too personal with me the way you just did, I usually run as fast as I can in the other direction. I'm scared to death of getting too involved with anyone. I don't want to lose my freedom."

"You don't have to lose anything. In fact, you'll discover that instead of losing, you actually gain."

"I don't want to take the risk."

"But what about John LaFerney? Don't you take risks there? Aren't you two involved?" He realized he was holding his breath as he waited for her answer.

"Not intimately. He knows how I feel, and it doesn't matter to him. We enjoy each other's company. He knows that if he ever tries to get too personal, it will ruin our friendship. He understands my reasoning and abides by the rules I go by."

"You have rules?"

"Yes, and if a relationship develops past a certain point, it's over. I withdraw and find someone else. I'm way too smart to let myself get that involved with anyone."

"You've got the wrong idea about love, and I guess I'll just have to be the one to prove it to you."

"Randy, I'm warning you," she began.

"Hey, I'm already making headway. You just called me by my first name." Leaning forward, he placed a warm, sensitive kiss on her cheek and then walked past her into the hall. That little moment of valor took all the strength he had. What he had really wanted to do was ravish her on the spot. Why did she have to be so complex?

"Where are you going?"

"Out to get more mistletoe. Besides, you've got things to think about. See you Sunday."

Sunday? That's right. Randy was coming over to help get the food ready for the family get-together that evening. Sighing, Leslie knew she would not have to put up with him again until then.

Suddenly Sunday seemed very far away.

Chapter Five

"Hey, over here!" Leslie heard as she stepped out of her car. Since it was such a lovely day, already in the upper fifties although it was so close to Christmas, she had not bothered to pull into her mother's garage but had parked in front of the house, near the front door. Glancing in the direction from which she had heard Randy's voice, she spotted him in the neighbor's front yard, playing with young Joey Jackson and his shaggy little dog.

"What are you doing over there?" she shouted as she headed in their direction. It was no surprise to her that Joey had latched on to Randy as he had. Joey used to pester Lucille just as often. Leslie had warned Randy well ahead of time, but he didn't seem to mind the little boy's daily interruptions at all. In a neighborhood that no longer had children, Joey was lonely when he was staying with his grandmother, which was most of the time. Joey's father had died two years ago, and his mother now worked full-time. Lately, too, she seemed to be putting in more and more overtime and making more company trips, thus having to leave Joey with his grandmother quite a lot.

"Playing while we wait for your mother to get home from church. She's late," Randy explained, then ordered Joey to head out for a pass. When the boy was far enough away, Randy threw the ragged football to him. Catching it with both hands and tucking it neatly to his skinny frame, the boy ran as fast as he could back toward Randy. It was obvious that the object of the game was to keep Barky from getting the ball. The dog seemed delighted at his part in the game and chased eagerly after the boy.

"Your turn," Joey gasped as he made it to Randy's side with a determined Barky hanging on to his jacket sleeve. Instantly, Randy took off and ran a short distance from the boy, holding his hands out for the pass. Catching the ball with ease, he dodged the excited dog and made it back to Joey unscathed.

"You want a turn?" Joey asked, looking up at Leslie.

"Oh, no, I'd better not. I'm not exactly dressed for football," she said, looking down at the black slacks and sweater she had worn. She had dressed for the family dinner, not a game of keep-away with an overactive dog.

"And I thought you were supposed to be some sort of pro. Just a lot of talk, huh?" Randy taunted her with narrowed blue eyes. He bore a good-natured grin that would have endeared him to even the coldest heart. "I bet you couldn't catch a football if you tried."

"It doesn't hurt none," Joey put in encouragingly.

Not one to ignore a challenge, Leslie took off running and told Joey to throw it to her. She would show them she could catch a football. When he did throw it and it flew over her head, she leaped up and made a spectacular catch. As she came back down on the ground ready to run it back in, she noticed that Barky had already headed in her direction. Running in a different direction from the dog's she also became aware that Randy was charging at her, too.

Banking a sharp turn, she made an attempt to run between them, but she failed miserably as they both seemed to reach her at about the same time, sending her sprawling into the dormant grass with scattered leaves and pine needles. The cool air filled with golden laughter as they tumbled together in a tangled heap. When they came to a stop, Leslie was very much aware that Randy lay on top of her and that Barky was jumping wildly about, growling with intent as he tried to wrestle the ball from her grip with his teeth.

Randy's crystal eyes were sparkling with delight as he said in a low, guttural voice, "Gotcha."

Trying to wiggle out from under him, Leslie saw that it was useless, and finally admitted that he indeed did have her. "And just what, pray tell, do you intend to do with me?"

His reply was a low growl accompanied by a long, meaningful look into her dark eyes. "I know what I'd like to do with you."

"And what's that?" she asked, widening her eyes innocently. Neither was aware that Barky had escaped victoriously with the ball. Neither cared.

"I'd like to make wild, passionate love to you."

"You are the victor—do what you wish." She felt safe enough with Joey just a few yards away. What she did not consider was that later on in the day she would not have the protection of the young chaperon. "I seem to be powerless against you."

"Hmm." It was obvious that he was speculating on what he would do if only they were alone. His eyes lingered on her smiling lips just a moment before traveling downward.

"Hey, you two, what's wrong?" Joey called out as he ran to find out why they were not getting up as they were supposed to—after all, Barky had the ball now.

"We were just discussing something," Randy said, rolling off and letting her up. "But I guess we can talk about it later."

Leslie gave him a wary look as she stood up and began brushing remnants of dead leaves and grass from her clothes. She gave out a startled gasp when Randy stepped forward and began assisting her, his hands sending tiny electrical charges through her system as they lightly grazed her clothing.

That was just the beginning of a very trying day for Leslie. Every time she ended up being alone with him, he would find a reason to touch her and taunt her, often suggesting another game of tackle football, only this time he felt they should play one on one in his bedroom. By the time the first of her mother's guests began to arrive that evening, Leslie was a nervous wreck.

The more she had warned him to behave himself, the more determined Randy had seemed to misbehave. True to his word, he had tacked mistletoe over every doorway in the house and had twice tried to take advantage of it. In both cases, she had barely escaped his unnerving kiss. In all honesty, Leslie had to admit to herself that she liked the game of pursuit he was playing as long as she kept coming out the victor in each of their skirmishes. It did mean staying superalert and on the defensive whenever he was around, and even when he wasn't. He seemed to have the ability to appear out of nowhere, and he was always ready to put the make on her.

That night, while Leslie lay in bed trying futilely to go to sleep, she discovered that once again she could think of little else than that insufferable Randy Brinnad. One of his idiotic jokes would come to mind and she would find herself smiling. She would remember his casual touch and feel her blood rush through her as her pulse jumped out of control. The man was definitely getting under her skin, and there was nothing she seemed able to do about it. What was worse, she wasn't sure she still wanted to do anything about it. She caught herself spending more and more time at her mother's. Her lunch hours seemed to stretch longer every day, in spite of her hectic schedule at work. By that following Friday, she was aware that she was actually enjoying Randy being around and was no longer interested in having him fired—but she still wasn't considering a serious relationship with him, either.

"Hey, I know a place that makes pizza even better than that," Randy told her as he gathered up the dirty lunch dishes. Somehow they had gotten on the subject of pizza, and Leslie had sung the praises of her favorite Italian restaurant. Margaret had gone upstairs to file a broken fingernail, leaving Leslie alone with Randy.

"Better than Antonio's?" Leslie asked skeptically.

"This pizza makes anyone else's taste like messy cardboard. It's so good it'll make your taste buds absolutely delirious."

"Where is this place?"

"Hey, I know—why don't I take you there tonight? You don't have any plans, do you?"

"No," Leslie admitted cautiously. "I don't have any real plans."

"And your mother's not going to be home tonight," he reminded her. "You'd probably just be eating alone. Why not spend the evening with me and let me treat you to the greatest pizza around?"

"You sure this pizza is the greatest?"

"There's none better."

"I know I'm going to regret this," she said slowly, realizing she was about to accept.

"Then it's a date?"

Cringing, Leslie replied, "Just for pizza. No dessert!" She glanced at him with a raised brow to make certain he caught the double meaning intended.

Laughing, Randy told her he'd pick her up at her apartment around seven.

It had never occurred to her that the place serving this incredible pizza would be his own house. She first became suspicious when they turned down a tree-lined residential street instead of a main highway leading into the city.

"Exactly what is the name of this place?" she frowned, looking ahead for any possible signs of a restaurant.

"I like to call it home, but most people just call it Randy's house."

"What are you up to?"

"You certainly are a suspicious woman." He laughed. "I told you, I'm taking you to a place that serves the best pizza around. Didn't I mention that I'm the one who makes it?"

"No, it must have slipped your mind."

"Must have," he said, nodding in agreement.

"Well, don't let it slip your mind that I'm just here for pizza," she warned him, straining to look ahead through the dimly lit darkness. In spite of the full alert she had just put herself on, she was actually becoming eager to see what his house was like. Something electrifying stirred inside her knowing that the evening had just taken a personal turn. She was going to be completely alone with Randy in his home. She would be able to get to know more about the man she realized she had a growing interest in.

"Just pizza. I'll see if I can remember that." He paused before adding, with a cockeyed grin, "I think I should be able to remember something as important as that. I'm very good at remembering things. Now what did you say your name was?"

Groaning aloud, Leslie let that one pass. She was more interested in the fact that they were slowing down and turning into a narrow drive. When his headlights panned across the small brick house, Leslie caught her first sight of Randy's home. It was larger and nicer than she had expected. The brick of the house, an L-shaped ranch-style building, was a mass of selected earth tones set off by black mortar and mahogany trim. The yard was uncluttered and well kept. The dark-green holly bushes that bordered the house were all uniform in size and kept trimmed at window height.

While she unfolded herself from the cramped confines of his coupe, he pulled up one of the garage doors, then led her through the darkened area to a windowed door. Once he had flipped on the garage light, she saw that he had several old cars in various stages of repair scattered across the large, two-bay area. Before she could ask about them, he had the door open and was bidding her welcome to his humble abode. Eagerly, she stepped inside to see just how Randy Brinnad lived. By now she had secretly admitted his ability to keep house, and was not really surprised to find that his home was immaculate.

The kitchen was the first room she got to see. There were appliances of all sorts, and although sparkling clean, the room looked definitely used. Next he led her through a small dining room to a large living area that centered around a huge rock fireplace.

"This room certainly seems to fit your nature."

"I hope that was intended as a compliment," he tossed over his shoulder as he knelt in front of the fireplace, adjusting the kindling before adding several large logs from a stack nearby.

"As close to a compliment as you're going to get," she said, laughing, then she glanced around while he worked to build a fire. The room was rugged and masculine, closely resembling a lodge of some sort. The walls were of rough, dark wood, and lantern-style fixtures dangled from large, exposed beams. Although the living area was carpeted, the other floors were of gleaming hardwood. The furniture was built from durable pine, upholstered with fabrics of different earth tones that blended smoothly. Smiling, Leslie openly admired the room, but in secret it was the man who had put it together she admired most. Her attention was focused on the broad-shouldered, narrow-waisted man in front of the fireplace. Although he was not bulging with muscles, her critical gaze noted that every inch of him was in fine shape.

"Why don't you make yourself comfortable here on the couch while I go into the kitchen and get the pizza under way?" he suggested moments after the fire was blazing. Motioning to the large Early American couch that was situated a comfortable distance from the fireplace, he waited until she had settled in before leaving her alone.

Unable to resist a little snooping while he was gone, Leslie was drawn to a set of double doors on the side of the octagonal-shaped end table near her. To her delight, she discovered several old scrapbooks inside, and she didn't hesitate to pull them out. Among the yellowing newspaper articles about a handsome young daredevil from Marshall, Texas, making all-district in football and all-state in baseball during his last two years of high school, she found pictures of a happy, always-smiling Randy at various stages of his life.

Several of the same faces kept appearing in many of the pictures, leading Leslie to believe they were his family. She guessed him to have a brother a few years younger than he, a sister even younger, and a happily married set of parents.

"Oh, no, you're not looking at those, are you?" she heard him groan when he returned. "I was such a goofy-looking kid."

"You weren't goofy-looking," she admonished, but glancing back down she had to admit he did look a little strange in some of the pictures. "You just looked different from the way you do now."

"I hope so," he said with a moan. "I like to think there's been quite a bit of change, and all of it for the better."

Looking at him and smiling, knowing she felt the same way about her own pictures during those awkward adolescent years, she assured him, "Yes, I think the change has been for the better."

Glancing down to the page she had been looking at and wincing noticeably, he complained, "Not that picture of me in those stupid bell-bottoms! Come on, let me put those away."

Reluctantly, having already seen most of them anyway, she let him take the scrapbooks from her and hide them back under the table. "I think you looked pretty good in those bell-bottoms. I agree that purple is not exactly your best color, but they looked all right. How old were you then?"

"Old enough to know better. About fourteen, I guess."

"I noticed most of those articles were from the *Marshall News Messenger*. Is that where you grew up? In Marshall, Texas?" Now that her curiosity was up, she was bursting with questions.

"If you are assuming I did grow up. Some people have their doubts," he retorted with a chuckle. "Actually, I lived in Marshall until I was nearly twenty."

"What made you want to move to Shreveport?"

"The town formed a special rail committee to run me out of town," he quipped. "I was no match for them."

"Randy, seriously, what made you want to move here?"

"A job mostly. Oh, and the fact that I was getting tired of the old hometown and getting a little restless for new adventures. So as soon as I'd finished two years of business administration at Kilgore College, I struck out on my own. I don't exactly know why I chose Shreveport. I guess I wanted my freedom, but at the same time I didn't want to live too far away from my family. I wanted to be able to go home for any special events that might crop up, and with my brother about to be a senior that year, I knew there'd be lots of special events I'd want to go to. So I went only as far as Shreveport and got a job working for Walls'n'Rae Tires."

"Walls'n'Rae Tires? What sort of work did you do there?" she prompted him. The more she learned, the more she wanted to know.

"I mostly kept books and worked the financial end at the main location on Spring Street, near the riverfront. I'm one of those guys who has a natural head for figures." He grinned devilishly, giving her own figure the once-over.

"Settle down," she warned him, then went on to ask some more questions. "If you're trained as an accountant, how'd you ever end up with the job you have now?"

"Walls'n'Rae closed down one of their locations and had to lay off a number of men. That last recession caught them pretty hard. I was one of the poor unfortunates they had to let go." He shrugged slightly. It was obvious he held no hard feelings.

"Okay, how'd you end up with Bellamy's?"

"You sure do ask a lot of questions," he observed. "When do I get to ask the questions?"

"Later, much later. Now how'd you end up working as a housekeeper?"

"Right after I'd been laid off, my aunt suggested I go to work for her housekeeping service, which is Bellamy's, to help pay my bills until I either got called back to work or could find an accountant's position somewhere else. Not one to want to collect unemployment, I agreed. That was two years ago, and I have yet to find a job that pays me better that I'd enjoy even half as much as I do this one. I actually like the physical labor and the different challenges I find with the job, so I've stayed with it. I never want to go back to a desk job. I'm just not the dormant type. I like to use my body as well as my mind. I need to be able to move around. It would take a job with lots of security and personal rewards to make me change now. I may get a lot of kidding about my job from my friends, but I'm happy doing what I do. As I see it, that's what matters most."

A loud buzzer sounded from the kitchen, and Randy hurried out of the room. Soon he reentered the dining area carrying a large rectangular pizza that sent a dizzying aroma through the room.

"Get it while it's hot," he chanted as he placed the steaming pizza between their plates on a hot pad that had already been placed on the table.

"Ouch, I didn't know it was still *that* hot," he yelped when the pad he had used to carry it slipped. "Hmm, eat at your own risk."

For the next half hour, they ate what turned out to be as good a pizza as Randy had boasted it would be.

Better. Leslie found that she could not stop even when her stomach told her that she had already reached her limit. By the time the pizza was all gone, she was in glorious pain. And when Randy suggested she grab her drink and follow him into the living room while they let their food settle, she could only moan her agreement and follow.

When Randy plopped down on the floor in front of the glowing fire and stretched out, leaning his back comfortably against the couch, Leslie frowned. She wasn't sure she was going to be able to join him. The thought of bending at the waist was not too appealing at the moment. What was worse, she was not at all sure she would ever be able to make it back up.

"It might be better if I sat on the couch. If I tried to get down there, I might not ever be able to get back up. My stomach feels like a lead anchor. If I made it to the floor, I might end up becoming a permanent fixture around here."

"That's okay by me—I promise to dust you regularly," he offered, patting the floor beside him. "Come on, you can make it if you really give it your best effort."

Groaning, she finally decided to give it a try and eased herself to the floor. She was wondering how she was ever going to fold herself into Randy's small car when the time came and still be able to breathe. Just thinking about it caused her unbearable misery. It might make better sense to rent a bus.

Once Leslie had settled in next to Randy, she was amazed at how comfortable sitting on the floor was in spite of her pizza-packed middle. The thick carpet cushioned her, and the couch offered her soft support. The gentle warmth from the fire and the sated feeling from within allowed Leslie to relax more than usual. For the first time she let her guard down completely and enjoyed a companionable moment with Randy. They talked about things that did not really matter, yet seemed nice to talk about. They discussed everything from their childhoods to current events. It was the first time Leslie could remember their being able to hold a civil conversation without her having to be wary of him, and the time passed quickly. Randy was behaving himself. It was not until Leslie mentioned how late it was getting and suggested she be going that he even made an attempt to touch her.

"Not yet," he pleaded, reaching out and gently caressing her cheek with the palm of his hand. Warm shafts of delight wafted through her. Oh, that felt good.

"Leslie, stay a while longer."

"But I have to go to work tomorrow. Not everyone gets Saturdays off, you know," she argued weakly. Her concentration was not on what she was saying, but on the sensitive touch of his hand. This time she did not pull away from him. She did not sense a reason to.

"Please stay," he said in a near whisper. "Please."

His eyes searched hers for a sign of withdrawal as he drew nearer to her. She felt mesmerized by the crystal-blue depths and did not protest when his lips claimed hers in a wondrously tender kiss. It was all she remembered his kiss could be. That same strange warmth invaded her, spreading through her like a hot mist and leaving her feeling intoxicated and weak. As she drifted onto some higher plane, she thought vaguely that if she hadn't known better she would have sworn he had been spiking her drinks all evening with some powerful potion.

Drawing his other arm around her, he slowly pulled her to him, and in the same moment he leaned forward, laying her gently on the floor and coming to rest more on top of her than not, his lips never leaving hers. As her body absorbed the pleasure of his passionate embrace, her mind had yet to issue an alarm. Her insides were a molten mass, yet a slight shiver passed along her spine when his lips left hers and teased a trail down her sensitive neck. The contrast caused her skin to prickle.

Randy's mouth continued to work its magic on hers, and in a lusciously demanding kiss, his tongue teased the outer edges of her lips until she parted them willingly and let him sample the intimate areas of her mouth. A hand slipped beneath her sweater and softly stroked the outer curves of her silk-covered breasts. While his kiss worked its wizardry, his fingers eased beneath her bra and lightly brushed the sensitive peaks straining to burst free. In an effortless movement, Randy unclasped the bra and moved quickly to grasp one of the swelling breasts he had released.

Leslie gasped aloud as her brain finally realized the danger and screamed its warnings. Hesitating, she moved a hand over his to stop his movements. The sensations she felt made her want to continue, to lose herself in the heated passions claiming her body, but what shred of sanity she was left with warned her that she could be heading into a relationship more serious than she could deal with. If she was to get too involved, come to care too much for this man, she would be lost. Urgently, she tried to sort out her priorities and her fears.

Randy sensed her hesitance and slowly eased his hand out from under her sweater. With deep concern in his crystal gaze, he pulled away from her and looked at her a long moment before speaking. "You're holding back. Most of you seems willing, almost eager, but a tiny part of you is holding back."

"I'm sorry," she said in a shaky voice. But it was true.

"Don't be," he said with a gentle smile. As he sat up, she could tell he was having as much difficulty in getting his breathing back under control as she was.

Sitting up beside him, she found it was hard to look him in the eye. Reaching behind her, she refastened her bra and hoped that he would speak again to relieve the shameful silence. She had no idea what more she could say other than that she was sorry. She felt like some sort of cheap tease, even though it had not been her intention to lead him on.

"I can wait until you're ready to give yourself freely. When and if you finally do give to me, I want it all. I don't just want your body, or the pleasure I'm sure you can offer me, I want all of you. I want your body, your heart and your very soul to be mine. And if I can't have all of you, I'd rather have nothing from you. That's the only way I consider us. For us it has to be all or nothing."

Leslie brought her gaze up to meet his. He was serious. He was no longer playing silly little games. He actually wanted her, all of her, but that was exactly what she had wanted to avoid, giving all of herself away like that and losing both her identity and her freedom in the process. She felt violently confused. Part of her wanted to reach out and tell him she was becoming very fond of him, that she had seriously considered making love to him, experiencing the ultimate with him, yet a tiny part of her still wanted to be protected from him and the power he might have over her if she were to give in to him. She could not decide which she wanted more. She wanted to cleave to him and know what it was like to make love with him, yet at the same time she wanted to run from him.

When she finally spoke, her voice was firmer than she had expected it to be. "Randy, I think I'd better go home now. Would you please take me home?"

"If you promise to think about what I've said."

"Oh, I'll think over what you said, all right, but I can't promise you what will become of any of it. I'm not sure I can give you all of me."

"Maybe not right now, but in time I think you will be able to. I'm willing to wait and see. Besides, what choice do I have? I'm in love with you." Standing up, he offered a hand to help her up. "And because I'm in love with you, I'm not about to give up. I'm going to do everything within my power to win you over. As I've already told you, I want you. I'll do my damnedest to have you."

Well, he was certainly being open and honest about it, which was a big plus in his favor. Some men had tried to sneak their way into her heart, and she had always shunned them because of it. This was new to her. She wanted to praise him for his frankness, his honesty, but decided against it, and against discussing the matter at all. But she could not help thinking about it as she rode back to her apartment in Randy's coupe.

Avoiding looking in his direction as he drove her home, she remained silent and watched the landscape roll by. It was not until they were near the complex that Randy's deep, mellow voice rose above the resonant roar of the finely tuned engine and claimed her attention.

"Tomorrow night I'm taking you dancing." It was a statement, not a question.

"Oh, are your sure about that?"

"You can dance, can't you?"

"I do all right."

"Good, then I'll pick you up around eight. Of course I plan to feed you first."

She looked over at him, expecting to find him gauging her for a reaction, but his eyes were scanning the driveway for a parking spot as they neared her apartment.

"Randy, didn't it ever occur to you that I might already have plans?"

"Well, do you?" Now he was looking at her.

"As a matter of fact, I have made tentative plans to go see a movie with John. We spend many of our Saturday evenings together."

"Is that what you'd rather do? See a movie with John?"

Thinking over his question a minute, she finally admitted, "No. I think I'd really rather go dancing with you."

"Then cancel out with John." He shrugged and looked away as he pulled into an empty space.

"I can't just call him up and say to forget our date," she protested.

"Why not? You'd rather be with me. You said so."

Heaving an exasperated breath, she thought that one over. She could very well call John and make excuses. After all, the date had never been officially confirmed. Comparing an evening at the movies with John to a possible night of dancing with Randy made her wonder if she shouldn't at least try to get out of the date with John. Still a tiny, almost indiscernible voice told her she would not feel right about it. John was her friend, and she could never treat a friend like that. "But I don't want to hurt his feelings. He's too nice a guy."

"Okay. Go on out to the movies with that too nice a guy, break my heart, but make it an early evening. I'm flexible, I'll still pick you up around eleven for a few glorious hours of dancing and what have you."

"You certainly have an answer for everything, don't you?"

He nodded. "Quick thinking—it's a gift. Besides, how am I going to win you over if I don't give you every opportunity to see how terrific I am?"

Leslie coughed good-naturedly, looking at him with a raised eyebrow as she reached for the door handle. "I hate to see such insecurity in a man. You really ought to do something to help build your self-confidence."

"Stop!" he shouted suddenly. "Don't move."

Leslie was so startled by his demand that she froze. Aware that he was hurrying to get out and around the car, she slowly turned her head and glanced out of the window beside her to see what had caused such a reaction in him. There was nothing out there that she could see but empty cars. What had caused Randy such sudden concern? Clasping her hands tightly together, she became aware of the apprehension forming in her throat. An icy chill gripped her. It wasn't until she saw the ridiculous grin he had pasted on his face as he gallantly opened the door and made a deep bow from the waist that she realized the only thing out there for her to fear was Randy himself.

"See what a terrific guy I am?"

Feeling the adrenaline drain out of her, she wanted to hit him. She wondered what he would look like wearing that silly grin in the back of his throat. Still, she had to laugh.

"Are you going to invite me in for a Coke, or maybe a friendly cup of robust-flavored international coffee? Now let me think. What flavor is right for this sort of thing?"

"And what sort of thing is that?"

"Royal seduction. What flavor coffee goes well with late-night royal seductions?"

"You're an idiot," she observed.

"Just because I don't know what flavor coffee to use? I'm devastated that you could be such a snob. We can't all be properly educated in the ways of coffee." Placing his hand over his heart, he bent his head remorsefully.

You may be devastated but you are also overacting." She shook her head and turned toward her apartment door. When she glanced back and saw that he was looking inquiringly at her, she sighed and waved him on. "Come on. One Coke, then out you go."

"You be a kind and generous woman, Leslie Lovall," he said in an attempt at a Scottish brogue. "I'll forever be beholden to ya. And if I ever be gettin' the chance, I'll be holdin' on to ya forever."

One thing could be said for Randy Brinnad—once he'd set his mind on something, he never let up.

Chapter Six

"Do I bother you?" Randy asked, overdoing his sweet expression of innocence.

"Since the day we met," she ground out, gritting between her teeth the small peppermint she had popped into her mouth right after lunch. Attempting once again to remain calm, she tried not to pay attention to the tingle his touch always caused her. The fellow was so exasperating. Narrowing her eyes, she added without looking down, "When I said you could help, I had in mind that you could hand me the light bulb after I got this one out."

"But you looked like you could fall off that chair and hurt yourself if someone didn't help steady you."

"You are not exactly a steadying influence, you know."

"That's always nice to hear."

"Look, if you want to steady something, steady the chair. I really don't need you to hold on to my legs like that," she said, shifting the mint from one side of her mouth to the other.

"If you want, I'll climb up there with you and steady your arms while you twist the bulb in," he suggested, grinning. With the worst of intentions, he allowed his hands to roam over her smooth, hosiery-clad legs. "My, but your lips are starting to twitch badly. Maybe I should climb up there and help you steady them. Be more than glad to."

It had been eight trying days since Randy had declared his intentions, and in those eight days he had tried every known means of seduction. He had taken her dancing, wined her, dined her, and brought her candy, flowers and a five-foot stuffed giraffe named Garrison. In fact, the only thing he had not done was serenade her at her window, and she hoped fervently that the idea would not occur to him.

Although she felt herself weakening on several occasions, she had yet to fall completely under his spell. Yet, in spite of her determination not to, she was growing more and more fond of him—admittedly, it was getting ever harder to hold on to her lifelong convictions. But she had yet to decide to commit herself fully to him. He pursued her shamelessly, and she responded by acting more annoyed than she really was. He was constantly getting too fresh, and she was always quick to reprimand him, although deep inside she knew she did not want him to stop. Theirs was an interesting relationship, to say the least.

While she was trying to concentrate on the task at hand and get her mother's light bulb changed, Randy's hands eased upward beneath the hem of her skirt, causing her to gasp in reaction. Suddenly the mint slid about halfway down her throat, and she had to cough several times in order to dislodge it so she could swallow it down.

"What's wrong?"

"I swallowed my mint. Thanks to you."

"Want me to get it for you?"

"Randy, don't you have something better to do than hold on to my legs while I try to change this bulb?"

"Actually, yes, I can think of something that would be much better than this," he answered smoothly. "Want to play some more tackle football? How about a little body wrestling?"

"How about letting me get on with this? I do have to get back to work, you know."

"Why didn't you just leave that for me to do? Are you trying to make me look bad? You wouldn't want me to lose my job, would you?"

"No," she said, realizing that at one time she had dearly wanted him to, but not anymore. "It's just that I'm used to doing such things around here. Lucille was scared to death of climbing on anything higher than a ten-inch footstool, and Mom has no business climbing up on chairs, either. She has bad balance. I've always been the one to change the ceiling bulbs around here."

"Well, now that I'm here I can handle the job," he commented, gazing intently at his hands as they gently stroked her shapely legs.

"I wish you *would* stick to handling your job and leave my legs alone. If you give me a run in my stockings, I'm going to put *your* lights out and see that they're never replaced."

Jerking his hands away, he scowled. "You just don't appreciate my good intentions."

"I know what your intentions are, and they would hardly be classified as good. Now take this bad bulb and hand me that new one."

"Yes, ma'am." He sounded like a dejected little boy.

When she looked down at him, he was wearing such a pout that she had to smile at it. He could be so cute when he put on his little-boy act. The worse his pout became, the bigger her smile.

Leslie realized that she had been finding reasons to smile more and more these days, and not just when Randy was putting on his antics. She caught herself smiling more at work, too. Her whole outlook had lightened. Although problems still occurred with over-whelming regularity, they did not seem to bother her nearly as much as they used to. If something went wrong, it went wrong. She would do what she could to rectify it, but she no longer dwelled on it. Her whole attitude had changed, and she was no longer as subject to those dark, moody periods in which she became un-bearable to have around. She had even shifted some of her work load to Cassie, which was what Cassie had been wanting her to do for quite some time now. That decision had not only freed more of her time, but had seemed to free her spirits as well. Actually, Leslie could not remember feeling this contented, this happy, in years.

"You do know I have plans for us this evening, don't you?" His voice broke into her reverie.

"I had a feeling you would. After all, you haven't missed a single evening in over a week. Why should I expect tonight to be any different? Since I can't seem to stop you, I'm trying to learn to live with it." It would

have disappointed her greatly if he hadn't had plans for
them. She could not bear the thought of an evening
alone or even an evening with John anymore. Everything paled in comparison with time spent with Randy.

"Well, don't you want to know what I have planned
for us?"

"I'm almost afraid to ask." Aware that Randy had
stepped back and was eyeing her legs eagerly, turning
his head slightly as if trying to better his view, she drew
her legs together self-consciously.

He shrugged. "Then let it be a surprise."

"No, I find your surprises a little unnerving. Just tell
me what to expect. Then I'll know how to dress."

"If we were to do what I'd really like to do, a slinky
silk nightie would be sufficient." That wicked smile she
had come to know all too well spread across his handsome face.

"Randall Edward Brinnad."

"Yes ma'am," he whimpered sweetly, again acting
like a little boy about to be punished but hoping to
avoid it.

"If you want to keep that mouth of yours located
somewhere below your nose, you'd better start behaving yourself."

He nodded. "Yes, ma'am." He sounded terribly in-
sincere.

Knowing there was no way her threats were going to
make him behave—they hadn't succeeded yet—she
shook her head with reluctant resignation. "Okay, just
what is it you have planned for tonight?"

"Can't tell you."

"Why not?"

"Because I want to keep my mouth where it is. I kind of like its present location."

Sighing heavily, she climbed down from the chair and allowed him to move it back to where it belonged. She knew she was smiling but tried to sound provoked when she said, "Maybe I should wear a suit of armor tonight, to be on the safe side."

Randy grinned at the thought.

Before she left to go back to work, Randy suggested she wear jeans that evening. Leslie spent the rest of the afternoon worrying about what he might have in mind. She would not put it past him to plan an evening at pig-wrestling matches or something of that nature.

That night she was only vaguely relieved when they pulled into the parking lot of a huge roller-skating rink. Skating had never been one of her stronger talents, but it was better than many of the things she had thought of in the course of the day.

"Randy, I haven't skated in ten years!" she protested as he turned off the ignition and reached for the door handle.

"Good."

"Why is that good?"

"You're going to need my supporting hand to help you get used to your skates. You're not afraid, are you?"

"To skate, no. Of you, yes. You just watch where that helping hand of yours decides to support me or I might just have to dismember your body," she warned before reaching for her own door handle.

In spite of the fact that they were the oldest couple on a floor filled mostly with preteens, Leslie had fun. It took several laps before she got accustomed to her skates and dared move away from the railing, but soon she was able to keep pace with the majority of the skaters.

She knew better than to try anything more daring than a spin or two and managed to stay on her feet most of the time. Only twice did she land rear end first on the hard floor and need Randy's assistance in getting up. She was not sure if her threats were finally beginning to work, or if it was because there were too many young eyes to witness it, but he kept his hands on respectable areas of her body at all times. But even having his hand resting lightly at her waist as they went around and around made her feel a little light-headed. It was crazy, the power Randy had in his touch.

As the evening wore on, she almost wished his hand would make a daring slip, but he remained a perfect gentleman the whole time they were at the rink. It was not until they were outside in the darkened parking area that the devil in him revealed itself again. As they walked toward his car, his hand began to move higher than her waist, boldly settling on the soft curve of her breast. Reacting quickly to the jolt it sent through her, Leslie raised her hand and popped him harshly on top of his head, rebuking him with the use of his full name. He looked at her with false indignation, then let a smile twitch the outer edges of his lips.

Finding a swarm of teenage boys standing around his car, Randy had to answer several questions concerning his three carburetors and high-rise manifold and the chopped roof before they would leave and he could finally help Leslie into the passenger seat. Again his helping hand was met by a terse slap. He was still rubbing the area she had slapped when he dug his keys out of his pocket and started the car. In pretending to be reaching for his floor shifter without looking, he grabbed her knee, gave it a decided squeeze—and got another sharp slap on his knuckles for his effort.

"Sorry," he coughed out. "Accident."

"Uh-huh." She sighed, knowing exactly how far from an accident it had been. "Now where to? Are you taking me back to my apartment?"

"Well, since you suggested it, why don't we go on back to your place."

"I didn't say *we*. I said *me*. Singular, not plural. Don't you know the difference?"

"I know that plural is more fun than singular," he pointed out. "You're not afraid to be alone with me in your apartment, are you?"

"Definitely."

"But why? You know what kind of guy I am."

"Exactly why. I *do* know what kind of guy you are."

When he started to turn on his little-boy pout, Leslie knew she had lost. She no longer wanted to win. She certainly was not ready for the evening to end any more than he was.

Warning him for the umpteenth time to behave himself, she finally agreed to prepare him a late-evening snack to munch on while they watched an old Hitchcock movie on television. Knowing there was a good chance he was not going to behave himself at all, she was fully preparing herself to do battle.

As expected, her warnings had gone unheeded. She managed to fight off his flirtatious advances while she prepared hot vegetable soup and sandwiches, and when they settled in on the couch, she made certain he was at arm's length.

Randy remained on his end of the couch while they ate, but about halfway through the movie he made his move and snuggled up close to her in the pretense of being frightened. When she eyed him suspiciously, ready to express her doubts, he claimed that Hitchcock movies had always scared him.

"When I was a kid, I was terrified to take showers alone and refused to ever dial anything with a first number corresponding to the letter M, and when the birds started to migrate in large multitudes, I immediately hid under my bed."

"I'm supposed to believe all this?"

Nodding his head vigorously, he said, "It certainly would be nice if you did. Especially the part about being afraid to take a shower alone. I thought you might volunteer to take one with me so I don't have to worry." Snuggling even closer, he smiled. "It certainly would be a nice gesture on your part."

"I thought I told you to behave."

"Have I done anything I shouldn't?" he asked, acting totally appalled by her insinuations. "I haven't reached out once and touched your hair like I've wanted to, have I?" he asked, lifting his hand to demonstrate by softly stroking the dark, shimmering tresses near her face.

He didn't wait for her to comment. "And I haven't run the back of my hand along your lovely face to enjoy the soft texture of your skin like I've wanted to, have I?" Gently, he allowed his hand to come down and trace the outline of her firmly set jaw. Again he did not give her time to respond with words, only with a tiny shiver. "And I certainly haven't dared to pull you close and kiss you like I've wanted to for so long."

Leslie found herself leaning willingly forward as he drew near for the expected kiss. As she did, a terrifying scream came from the direction of the television, but the only sound Leslie was interested in was the low moan welling up in her own throat. She decided she would allow them one kiss. What danger could there be in one little kiss? Lifting her arms to encircle his neck, she was determined to get the most from it. After all, there would be only one. That was all.

Although her original plan had been for them to share only that one kiss, when they actually came together her reaction was so intense that Leslie felt her resolve slowly melt away. Her senses began to swim in the warm tide of sensations that only Randy could elicit. She marveled at the uncanny ability he had to arouse her most sensual emotions. Maybe one kiss wasn't enough after all. Maybe she should consider letting him have another. What could it hurt?

Responding fully, she ran her hands down the firm muscles of his back. The excitement that came from simply touching him was undeniable, and she pressed her hands harder against him. He responded by tightening his own hold on her.

His lips became bolder in their possession of her lips, and his tongue plunged into the sweet depths of her mouth. She did not know how, but his wondrous power over her seemed to grow with each of their encounters. It was going to be next to impossible to pull away from him this time—and she wasn't even sure she wanted to. It was as if her inner voice was fading into the far distance, a faint echo of what it once had been. She now realized how much she wanted to make love to Randy. If only she could be sure she wouldn't fall in love with him in the process and become bound to him in some intolerable way.

She was so absorbed in what she was feeling and the thoughts those feelings provoked that she wasn't aware of what he said when he pulled away from her until he said it a second time. "Leslie, are you willing to give all of yourself to me yet? Or is there still a tiny part of you that's holding back? Do I have all of you?"

"I—I'm not sure. I do like the idea of making love to you . . ." Her voice paused in midthought.

"But you're not sure you want to surrender your heart to me. That's it, isn't it?"

Leslie looked beyond him to the black-and-white images on the television. It was just the movement that drew her gaze; her mind was on what was happening inside of her.

"I've already explained how I feel about letting any man control my heart or my life, and in all honesty, I do still feel slightly resistant to the idea of surrendering my heart completely. But if I ever do decide to, I know you'd be the only man I'd ever consider," she said, hoping he would understand. "It has nothing to do with whether or not I want to make love to you or whether or not I care for you. I just want to be secure in my freedom to do as I choose with my life. I don't want any emotional commitments. My independence is important to me."

"You might be willing to make love as long as there are no real commitments, but I'm not. I told you. With us, it has to be all or nothing. I won't settle for anything less." Having said that, he pulled completely away from her. "Leslie, I think I should be going."

She felt suddenly cold and empty. "No, don't," she pleaded. "Randy, please. Don't give up on us yet." Her words surprised even herself.

Standing, he gazed down at her and smiled.

"Oh, I have no intentions of giving up. I'll just have to try harder is all. I'm determined to make you mine. But not tonight." Leaning forward, he placed a warm kiss on her pensive forehead, then turned to leave. Valor was certainly getting harder to come by.

Relieved that she had not lost him entirely, at least not yet, Leslie jumped up and walked with him to her apartment door. She was not only confused, she realized, she was angry with herself for not being able to let go of her heart. She knew that if she ever lost his attention, she would be miserable. She loved it, and for the first time, as she gently closed the door behind him, she wondered if she might not be falling in love with more than the attention she was getting. Could she possibly be falling in love with the man? It was certainly something to think about, and that is all she did as she got ready for bed and eased into a fitful sleep.

It was Monday morning before Leslie saw Randy again. Although he called her twice on Sunday, he did not invite himself over as he usually did. During his second call, she herself suggested he come over and try out some of the chocolate fudge she was making, but he declined the invitation. She did not tell him that she rarely cooked anything, and the only reason she was bothering with the fudge was to keep herself occupied. She missed him dreadfully and was worried that, in spite of what he had said, he just might be giving up on her. And who could really blame him?

She felt as though she were walking on a lake covered with a sheet of thin ice as she entered her mother's kitchen from the walkway off the garage early Monday morning. She was nervous about facing Randy again, and she hoped that he hadn't changed toward her. She was very relieved when he appeared through the far door as she entered and he quickly offered to help her off with her coat. His hands still grazed her intimately when he eased back the lapels of the coat, and the old familiar flicker was still apparent in his crystal eyes. She felt tears well up in her own eyes. He had not given up at all. He was still interested.

Indeed, she soon found Randy fulfilling his promise to try even harder. He not only took advantage of every situation she left open to him, but he began to create his own situations, where he could either taunt her with provocative ideas or tease her with intimate touches. Only now she didn't pretend to be quite as annoyed as before. She still slapped his hands away, but not with the same vigor she had used before.

As the days counted down to Christmas, Leslie found herself on the first floor of Lovall's looking around for something special for Randy. She wanted to surprise him, but the gift had to be as unique as he was. She wished she had time to have a pair of purple bell-bottoms made, but Christmas was now only three days away.

Harlequin reaches
into the hearts and minds
of women across America
to bring you

Harlequin American Romance.™

Enter a uniquely American world of romance with

Harlequin American Romance.™

Harlequin American Romance novels are the first romances to explore today's new love relationships. These compelling romance novels reach into the hearts and minds of women across America... probing into the most intimate moments of romance, love and desire.

You'll follow romantic heroines and irresistible men as they boldly face confusing choices. Career first, love later? Love without marriage? Long-distance relationships? All the experiences that make love real are captured in the tender, loving pages of *Harlequin American Romance* novels.

What makes American women so different when it comes to love? Find out with this special *Harlequin American Romance* offer!

Send for your four free introductory books and tote bag now.

Get these Four Books and Tote Bag
FREE!

MAIL TO:
Harlequin Reader Service
2504 West Southern Avenue
Tempe, Arizona 85282

YES!
I want to be one of the first to discover
Harlequin American Romance. Send me FREE and without
obligation my four free books and FREE tote bag. If you
do not hear from me after I have examined my four FREE
books please send me four new *Harlequin American
Romance* novels each month as soon as they come off the
presses. I understand that I will be billed only $2.25 per
book (total $9.00). There are no shipping or handling
charges. There is no minimum number of books that I
have to purchase. In fact, I may cancel this arrangement
at any time...and keep the four introductory books and
tote bag FREE, without any obligation.

154 CIA NA3N

Name	(Please Print)

Address	Apt. No.

City	State/Prov.	Zip/Postal Code

Signature (If under 18, parent or guardian must sign.)

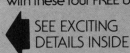
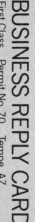

BUSINESS REPLY CARD

First Class   Permit No. 70   Tempe, AZ

POSTAGE WILL BE PAID BY ADDRESSEE

Harlequin Reader Service
2504 West Southern Avenue
Tempe, AZ 85282

NO POSTAGE
NECESSARY
IF MAILED
IN THE
UNITED STATES

Not really able to come up with any other brainstorms, she settled on an extremely large metal chest with several drawers of various depths in which to store mechanics' tools. She remembered having seen tools scattered over his garage floor, and had also noticed many stored in shallow cardboard boxes on his workbench. Knowing how he loved to have things organized, she felt he would really like the tool chest. It wasn't purple bell-bottoms, but it would do.

Leaving the clerk with orders to have it wrapped and delivered to her office, she returned to her desk and phoned Randy at her mother's house. Since he was not supposed to work at all on Christmas Eve and was no longer demanding every spare minute she had, she wanted to make sure she would see him so she could give him his present. If he had plans to go home to Marshall, which she suspected he did, she wanted to know when he would be going so she could get the present to him before he left.

Just as she had predicted, Randy did have plans to go home for the holiday. He had talked with his mother that very morning and promised he would arrive around midafternoon on the twenty-fourth.

"I told her I'd bring a big turkey for her to roast Christmas Day. Do you want to go with me?"

Leslie gave the phone a piercing look, which was traditionally a warning for him to be very careful about what he said next, even though she knew he could not benefit from her expressions over the phone. "Was that a shot of some sort? Are you insinuating I'm a big turkey?"

"Now, whatever gave you such an idea?" he said,

laughing. "I just thought it would be nice to have you go along. Really, it would please Mother to meet the girl who has finally stolen my heart. I've already told her all about you. She thought I was a confirmed bachelor. That I would never fall in love."

The invitation was tempting, especially upon hearing his less-than-subtle redeclaration of love, but she knew it would leave her own mother alone for most of Christmas Eve. Although her mother would go visit at her sister's in nearby Bossier City, which was just across the Red River, on Christmas Day, she would have nowhere to go and nothing much to do most of the night before. Then there was Carol to consider, too. Since they were young girls, they had exchanged their gifts on Christmas Eve. No doubt, Carol and her mother would be stopping by for the traditional eggnog and exchange of presents. Leslie would hate to disappoint them. Besides, she would hate to miss it.

"Actually, I'd like to meet the woman who is to blame for you turning out the way you have, but I can't. My plans are to be with Mom that evening. We always exchange our gifts on Christmas Eve. She's expecting me to be here. So is Carol."

"How about Christmas Day? I wasn't sure I was going to ask, being the sort of fellow that can't stand true rejection, but would you like to drive over and meet my family sometime Christmas Day? I really hate the thought of not getting to see you until the twenty-seventh." Randy had both the day before and the day after Christmas off.

Leslie didn't like the thought of having to go all that time without their seeing each other, either. But the idea of meeting his family made her extremely nervous, yet at the same time she was curious to discover what sort of family Randy had. Knowing she would be free after her Aunt Beulah's traditional Christmas lunch, she would be able to be in Marshall by midafternoon—that is, if Marshall wasn't too far away. She could then spend the rest of the day with Randy and his family.

"Are you sure your mother won't mind the intrusion on such a special family day?" she asked hesitantly.

"Mother would love it. But I'll warn you now. She's wanted to marry me off ever since I got out of college. She won't be subtle in her hints.

"I think I can handle that. I just might come, but only for a few hours. I'll have to work the next day, and the twenty-sixth is the worst, with returns and all. What should I wear?"

"Women," he muttered. "If you must wear something, make it clothes."

Seeing that he was not going to be much help to her in that area, she changed the subject. "Just how far is it to Marshall?"

"About an hour's drive. Why don't you see if Carol can come with you to keep you company on the way over, especially if you plan to come back that night? Actually, I think Carol, being so carefree and easygoing, is just the thing to help bring my brother out of his depression. Ever since his wife died a couple of years ago, he really gets depressed during the holidays. No one can stay depressed around Carol."

That was true enough. As witty and happy as Carol

always was, it eventually rubbed off. Leslie could not count the times Carol had brought her out of dark, dismal moods. Besides, it might make her feel more at ease if she had Carol around for support when meeting Randy's family. "I'll see what Carol's plans are."

"But if she can't come, don't *you* use it as an excuse not to come."

Leslie fingered the telephone cord nervously. None of this had solved the problem of getting his present to him. How could she word it so it wouldn't sound like a come-on? "I need to see you before you go. I have a gift for you. Or would you rather I bring it with me Christmas afternoon?"

"A present? For me?" She could hear the little-boy quality in his voice. "Heck, no, I don't want to have to wait. How about tomorrow night? Why don't I prepare another of my specialties and then we can open our gifts afterward?"

"I have a better idea. Since you've already had to cook for me so many times, why don't I do the cooking? Why don't you come over to my apartment around eight tomorrow night?"

"What about tonight? That would be even better."

"No, I need tonight to get things ready. I hate to admit it, but except for a pound of chocolate fudge, I don't have enough food in the house to feed a starving ant right now."

"Why don't I come over and help you get things ready?" Randy suggested.

"No, Randy, I don't really need any help."

"No charge."

"I'll just bet."

Leslie knew she would spend all her time enjoying his company and get very little done. She wanted that night to be special. Assuring him that his help was not necessary, she convinced him to stay away until the following night.

On her way home that evening, Leslie stopped off at the supermarket and bought all the things she would need to make tomorrow's supper. Knowing her apartment lacked holiday luster, she also purchased a small evergreen tree, several boxes of ornaments and a couple of strings of colored lights. As she led the heavily ladened sack boy out of the store, she realized she was singing a lively Christmas carol. What amazed her most was that she was not even aware she knew all the words to the song, and here she was well into the third stanza.

When she opened the trunk lid so the boy could place the two overflowing sacks and the small tree inside, she realized that the song was one of those Randy liked to sing. Evidently she had picked up the words from him. The thought of Randy singing carols as he worked warmed her in spite of the thirty-degree temperature outside.

"Thank you, and Merry Christmas," she told the sack boy with a jubilant smile, tipping him generously before she got back in the car.

Leslie worked as if she had wings while she moved a table and chair to make room for her first Christmas tree in front of the large bay window. She wanted everyone that passed her apartment to be able to admire the tree. In a little while she was already plugging in the lights and admiring her own handiwork. The tree may have been small, but what it lacked in size it made up for in beauty.

Next she went to work in the kitchen. She put away her purchases and dug out the utensils she would need, planning to get as much as she could done tonight so she could spend as little time as possible in the kitchen the following night. Once everything was prepared and stored in the refrigerator, she cleaned up the area until it seemed to sparkle. After all, the guy was a professional when it came to cleaning.

As she worked, her thoughts kept straying to Christmas Day. She wondered what his family was going to be like. The more she thought about the impression she would make on them, the more worried she became. Knowing she'd feel better about it if she could be sure Carol would be going with her, she stopped what she was doing and called her friend. She'd only halfway expected Carol to be home, and was very relieved when she answered.

"Merry Christmas," Leslie greeted her friend.

"Merry Christmas," Carol replied hesitantly, wondering why Leslie sounded so cheerful.

"Do you happen to have any special plans for Christmas Day?"

"No, nothing in particular, I'm afraid." Carol spoke cautiously. "Why?"

"Want some?"

"Some what?"

"Special plans for Christmas Day, of course."

"Depends." Carol was not about to commit herself until she had the facts.

"Randy wants me to drive over to Marshall to meet

his family, spend the afternoon, and have supper with them. He suggested I invite you to keep me company on the long drive over and back.''

"But what you really mean is that you are more than a little apprehensive over meeting his family, and you want someone supportive to help see you through it," Carol surmised.

"Exactly." Leslie laughed. She never could hide her true feelings from Carol. "But Randy was the first to suggest that you come, so will you do it?"

"Sure. I'd be glad to have somewhere to go Christmas Day, and I'll even do my best to ease some of the tension when you meet his family. What are friends for?"

"Thanks, I appreciate it. Will you be ready by two? I hope to leave about that time."

"I think I can manage that. What'll I wear?"

Remembering Randy's retort, she quickly responded, "Clothes would be nice."

"Thanks—I'll keep that in mind."

Once she and Carol had finalized their plans and she had hung up, her heart leaping at the thought that she would be entertaining Randy alone in her apartment the next evening, she turned her attention to the rest of the apartment.

Although she had never really cared what most people thought of her or her apartment, feeling they could take her or leave her the way she was, she did care what Randy thought of her. She worked at cleaning and straightening until nearly midnight, making the place look perfect. The next day she would only have to worry about making her bed before work and being sure she looked her very best by eight o'clock.

To her amazement, maybe for the first time in her life, she was ready far ahead of time. By seven o'clock that next evening she was completely prepared, dressed in the flowing, dark-brown jumpsuit she had bought just for the occasion. She had chosen the dark color because it brought out the highlights of her hair, which she had chosen to wear down and brushed away from her face. With its daring neckline and fitted waist, the outfit complemented her trim figure quite well. She hoped Randy would like it.

The extra time weighed heavy on her. There was absolutely nothing for her to do to occupy that last hour but wring her hands and pace the floor. She tried calling Carol for a chat to help pass the time, but there was no answer. Anxiously, she paced the carpeted floor until every time she came into contact with anything metal she popped with electricity. The tiny shocks, coming when she leasted expected them, only served to make her more fidgety.

When Randy finally showed up, right on the hour, she was so glad he was there that she flung the door wide and reached out to embrace him. Still electrically charged, she shot tiny blue sparks when they touched. "Wow! What a woman," he remarked, his eyes opening wide. "I want more of that."

Kicking the door shut behind him, he tossed the gift he was carrying onto a nearby table and pulled Leslie to him, emitting a low growl just before giving her a fierce kiss. This time the sparks were inside her.

"Is that how you always greet your hostess?" she gasped, trying to calm her erratic heartbeat.

"Only the really sexy ones," he commented as he

shrugged out of his coat. Underneath the coat he was wearing dark-blue slacks and a light-blue pullover shirt that was banded at the waist, which focused attention on his tapered body and broad shoulders.

Only the really sexy ones? Sexy? Leslie thought the words sounded a little foreign when she heard them used to describe her—she had never really thought of herself as sexy before. Suddenly she felt very sexy—and still very nervous.

To Leslie's relief, the meal went well. She did not burn anything, which she'd always tended to do in the past. Randy had seconds, not only of the prime ribs, but of the stuffed potatoes and broccoli spears as well, and that pleased her very much. After they finished, he helped her carry the dirty dishes to the sink, and when she complained that he was the guest, he claimed it was a habit he couldn't break.

Returning to the living area, he retrieved the forgotten present he had brought and placed it under the tree next to the huge one already there. He eyed the large package curiously as he settled in one corner of the couch. Leslie joined him, sitting next to him rather than at the other end as she usually did. For some reason she was in the mood to be close to him. Very close.

"When do I get to see what you got for me?" he asked, raising an arm and placing it behind her. His eyes left the package long enough to give her an inquiring look.

"You can open it now, if you want."

That was all the encouragement he needed. Hopping up, he went over and knelt beside the box, which looked enormous next to the one he had brought.

There was that little boy coming out again. Eagerly, he tossed the bow aside and began peeling back the colorful red paper.

"Well, aren't you going to come open yours?" he asked, pausing momentarily.

"Do I dare?" she asked before getting up to join him in front of the tree.

She had been so content to watch him that she had forgotten all about the gaily wrapped gift he had brought. Her curiosity now aroused, she sat on the floor beside him, her feet tucked under her, and reached for the gift.

"It isn't very heavy," she noted when she lifted the box high. Cautiously, she jiggled it. "And it doesn't rattle or tick...."

She removed the lovely bow with care and laid it aside. Randy, meantime, had revealed the unmarked cardboard box that concealed his gift. Noting the determined frown on his face, she paused and watched as he pulled the stapled top apart. It made her smile to see his determined face light up when he realized what was inside. Finding it easier to tear the cardboard away than to lift the chest out of the box, he was inspecting the drawers and compartments in a matter of seconds.

"Oh, Leslie, this is great! You shouldn't have spent this much." He went on to try the lock to see if it really worked. "Terrific!"

Leslie turned her attention to the package that still rested in her lap. Randy watched her, having scooted over so he could sit right beside her.

"I hope you like it. I know it's something you don't already have."

Noting the delighted sparkle in his blue eyes, Leslie grew suspicious again. She leaned away from what appeared to be an oversized shoe box just in case it was something that could attack when she lifted the lid off. Narrowing her dark eyes in readiness, she took a deep breath and yanked the lid away. Nothing jumped out.

Peering in, she found herself fighting back tears. There it was, just what she had asked for all those years—a real professional football. Although her days of running out and playing with the neighborhood boys were over, she treasured the thought of finally getting her football. He could not have thought of a more perfect gift.

"Oh, Randy, I love you," she burst out impulsively, then gasped as she realized what she had just said. The words had just popped out, surprising her as much as they did him. What didn't surprise her, though, was when Randy gathered her in his arms and held her close. He pressed her head against his strong shoulder, and she could feel his warmth against her cheek.

This time it was Leslie who pulled away just far enough to be able to maneuver a kiss. Her lips came to his as if they suddenly belonged there.

Chapter Seven

Randy met her kiss eagerly. She could feel his arms tighten around her in response, making her aware of how much he wanted her. He let out a low primitive growl, and his tongue dipped deeply into her mouth, tantalizing the area within. When the tongue retreated, Leslie boldly allowed hers to follow.

Leslie closed her eyes the better to allow her other senses full reign of her body. She was aware of the strength in Randy's arms as he held her close, noted the gentle fragrance of his cologne mixed with his own natural scent. While his lips continued to work their undeniable magic, she felt his fingers exploring her back, then move to the sensitive area along her rib cage. The expected warmth spread through her like a rolling gulf tide, bringing her untold pleasure—and, strangely, she felt absolutely no desire to resist his advances. In fact, she welcomed them as she never had before.

She was consumed with her passion, almost delirious with it. A slow burning sensation centered itself in the very pit of her stomach and reached out to all of her intimate places. She had never felt such a stinging, blistering need.

"Randy—" His name was but a soft moan from her lips.

Grasping his shoulders, she pulled herself against him with all her might. She wanted him closer, somehow to mesh with him, to become a part of him. She had never known such intense emotion in her life. She truly ached with her desires, knew without any question that only Randy had the power to bring her any relief.

As Randy's masterful hands stroked the sensitive areas along the sides of her breasts, they brought new feelings of desire to her. He wedged one hand between her breasts and made contact with the sensitive peaks that had been straining against him. Leslie was lost to these powerful feelings. It was as if Randy had slipped into her heart and now possessed her very soul. She needed to slake her desires, to meet her needs—and only Randy could appease the fire burning inside her. She needed, demanded, relief from the wildfire raging within. She pressed against him in order to let him know her urgency.

A tremor passed through Randy so strong that even Leslie felt it just before he pulled his lips free of hers. Gasping for breath, he moved his hands to her shoulders and abruptly pushed himself away from her. He pressed his eyes shut and took several deep, uncontrolled breaths.

"What's wrong?" she asked. Everything in her felt as though it were ablaze. She was confused—why was he not willing to release her from this torment?

"We need to talk," he muttered. His chest was still heaving with his determination to control himself.

"Talk?" Here she was ready to make love to him, and he wanted to talk?

"Yes, talk. Leslie, I love you more than I ever knew I could love a woman. It sounds crazy, but I love you so much that I can't *make* love to you until I know for certain that you return my love in full. Remember? I told you that I had to have all of you or nothing? If I were to make love to you and then discover it was just a physical need on your part, I wouldn't be able to stand it. I've got to have a commitment from you. A definite commitment. With you it could never be a casual relationship, a momentary fling. You're different from any woman I've ever known. It can only be a serious bond for us, and it must be a bond that will last forever. I can't live with anything else."

Leslie's mind was racing. Did she actually love him or did she want him simply because he had awakened desires in her she had never felt before? The physical need was apparent, as was the fact that she cared deeply for him, but was this special feeling she felt for him love? Could she really commit herself to him? She had never felt this strongly about any man before, but *was* it love? How could she be sure?

"Randy, I—I—"

"That's all the answer I need. You're still hesitant. You're still holding back what I want most of all. Your heart. Damn, why can't you love me the way I love you? I'm willing to give you time, but how much time will it take? I may go raving mad with my desire for you before you decide one way or the other about me."

He raked his hands through his hair, and for a moment it looked as though he wanted to cry out in frustration. "Tell me one thing, Leslie. Is there a chance that you might grow to love me or am I wasting my time? Am I headed for a fall?"

"I don't know. I'm confused. I'm very fond of you. I find myself thinking about you all the time. When I'm not with you, I miss you dreadfully and can hardly wait until I'm able to see you again. I find myself thinking about your kiss, remembering your smile, and wondering what it would be like to make love to you—and until you mention a promise of forever, I'm all in favor of an intimate relationship with you."

"But I want more than a relationship with you. Don't you understand? I want to marry you. I have to have promises. I want you to be the one who bears my children, who helps me through hard times, who burns my toast in the morning. I want you beside me when I grow old and can only talk about what great times we had. I want somebody to share my memories and my underwear drawer."

"Marry? You want to marry me?" A smile spread across her face. He wanted to marry her. Although she had always been opposed to marriage for herself, the thought of it suddenly brought her great pleasure. There were certain aspects of being a wife and mother that were actually appealing when she considered Randy in the role of husband.

"That's what forever is all about. I don't want a temporary affair with you. I'm not simply after your gorgeous body, although the thought of making love to you drives me into a wild frenzy; I want *you*. All of you.

I need you to love me just as much as I love you. Totally and completely. Forever."

This had to be the most maddening conversation she had ever held. Nothing pleased her more than to know that Randy loved her and honestly wanted to marry her, but nothing scared her as much as the thought of becoming someone's property, always being at someone's beck and call. She wanted Randy more than she had ever known possible, but did she love him? Looking at the dark misery so evident in his eyes made something inside her ache. She did not want to hurt him—not Randy, not this sweet, lovable, overbearing source of total aggravation and wonder. She cared too much for him. But did she really love him?

"Hey, I'm not trying to force you to make a decision about me right now," he said, sensing her quandary. "After all, we've only known each other a few weeks, but to me it seems as if I've always known and loved you. I'm willing to wait until you come to realize what a great and wonderful person I am. After all, how long can that take?" Suddenly his tone was light again. Although his face seemed drained, he pasted a smile back in place and wanted to know if she still had any of that fudge she was supposed to have made Sunday.

For the rest of the evening he was not the same lighthearted Randy she was used to. He kept the tone of conversation impersonal yet friendly, but his perpetual smile no longer reached the crystal depths of his eyes, and Leslie knew she was to blame. She had to come to terms with what she felt before she really hurt him. If she didn't truly love him, she shouldn't keep letting him hang on to his hopes, and if she did indeed love him, he needed to know that, too. She needed to know. But how would she find out if what she felt was love?

Because the tool chest was too big to fit into Randy's car, he asked if he could leave it there until he came back from Marshall on the twenty-sixth. She would have offered to deliver it to his house while he was gone, but decided she would rather wait until he could come for it. She wanted to be sure he had a reason to come see her in case her inability to declare her love caused him to be reluctant in doing so. She was relieved that he still wanted her to come and meet his family. His last words as he gave her a brief good-bye kiss on the cheek were "See you Christmas Day."

"I'll be there with Christmas bells on."

ALTHOUGH THE TWENTY-FOURTH was hectic at Lovall's, all Leslie could do was think of Randy. She found herself missing him even before he left the city. Many times Cassie had to literally clap her hands to get her boss's full attention. Leslie felt a dull emptiness in the pit of her stomach, and she was not even sure why. It wasn't as if Randy had said he was giving up on her— he hadn't told her to take a flying leap off the nearest tall building—so why did she feel so desolate? For all the good she was doing, she thought, she might as well have stayed at home in bed. Emotions. Why did they have to get in the way of reason?

She felt little of the seasonal cheer that evening when Carol and her mother dropped by for their traditional eggnog and to exchange presents. Although Carol's mother, Beth Clifton, and Margaret Lovall had always been close friends, they had grown closer since

Beth's husband died, just months after Margaret's husband died, the mutual sense of loss bringing them closer together. Their special friendship was evident when they shared the special moment of Christmas.

Leslie tried to show the proper mood as she opened her gifts, but Carol was not fooled. The first opportunity she had to talk with Leslie alone, she asked, pointblank, "What on earth is wrong with you?"

"Nothing, I'm just tired," Leslie answered, trying not to let Carol get a clear view of her eyes. Carol had a way of seeing right through to her very soul.

"Come on, out with it."

Leslie was reluctant to talk about any of it, but once Carol got her started, she poured out everything to her friend. She even admitted her confusion as to what she really felt for Randy, and how all day she had felt a numbing despair that rendered her brain useless.

"Oh, my!" Carol grinned. "I never thought I'd see the day."

"What day? Don't be so obscure. If you have something to say, just come out with it," Leslie demanded, eyeing her blond friend suspiciously. She was in no mood for theatrics.

"I never thought I'd see the day when Leslie Lovall would actually be in love."

"Love?"

"Sure—it's written all over you. You're in love and scared to death of it."

"Me?"

"Sure, you're confused, insecure, in heart-wrenching agony over how he feels, terrified he might stop feeling at all. You have an overpowering need to cry and don't even know why. Isn't it grand?''

"No, it feels like hell."

"That's love, all right."

Her first thought was to deny it, but when she opened her mouth to voice her denial, it did not come. She simply stood there with her mouth open, thinking over what Carol had said.

"Then why do so many people strive so hard to find love if it makes them feel so horrible?" It did not make very much sense to Leslie.

"There are two sides to love. Right now you're struggling with the darker side of love. The good side is the great feeling you have whenever you're with that special someone, the warmth that can stay with you when things are right between you. It's being so happy you think you could burst with joy. It's only when things are not going exactly right that all the dreadful aspects of love come out. I wish I was in love again. Love is especially wonderful during the holidays. It's been so long since I've really felt the wonder of being in love. I'd give anything to trade places with you and be suffering through the initial growing pains of love, knowing what might develop."

Leslie forgot all about the diet cola she had come into the kitchen for as she thought over what Carol had just said. "But if I am in love, as you say, then why don't I want to commit myself to him? Why am I still so afraid of giving up my independence?"

"I don't have the answer to that one. I know how opposed you are to allowing anyone to tell you how to run your life. How you're so afraid of ending up like your mother, especially the way she was right after your father died. You have some odd notion that marriage takes away a woman's ability to function. Heaven knows how many fights we've had because of it. But I would think being in love with the guy would make the difference in the way you see things. Actually, you should be eager to share your life with him and be willing to give up part of your freedom, considering what you'd be getting in return. Maybe he's right."

"How's that?"

"You just need a little time. It's simply too new to you right now. Give yourself time to let your brain and your heart sort everything out." Carol giggled as she listened to herself. "Don't I sound like the wise old sage?"

Actually, Carol did seem to be offering sound advice. Usually Leslie took anything Carol had to say with a grain of salt, because of her strange views on life, but this time she felt her friend was right. Given more time, maybe she would be able to sort out all her confused feelings. Maybe she was in love with Randy. The thought of being in love seemed more pleasing than it ever had before. If only love did not automatically come with strings and attachments!

In sharp contrast to the previous week, Christmas Day was bright and sunny. The temperature had reached the midsixties by noon, and there was hardly a cloud in the sky. As soon as Leslie could, she slipped away from her Aunt Beulah's and headed for Carol's. She burned with excitement and curiosity, knowing her destination was Randy's parents' home. Although she was still nervous at the prospect of meeting his family, she was anxious to be with Randy and to learn more about him. She was also relieved to know that Carol would be there. She would have been terrified meeting Randy's family alone. What if they did not like her?

During the ride over, Carol helped her keep her mind off her apprehensions. She kept the conversation light and flowing about silly things that did not matter. By the time Leslie had spotted the Marshall/Jefferson exit off I-20, a little before three o'clock, they were giggling over another in a long line of Carol's outlandish ideas.

Having handed Carol the map Randy had drawn for her, Leslie followed the directions as Carol read them and amazed them both by driving directly to Randy's parents' house. It was right on the outskirts of Marshall, just as Randy had said it would be.

"This is the place," she said, taking a deep breath. Her eyes scanned the six-acre site, noting the mixture of huge broadleaf trees, with a few amber leaves still clinging to their branches, and tall pines, which seemed that much more green by contrast. Off to one side was a large patch of torn earth that indicated where a vegetable garden had been. A small barnlike structure lay just beyond the garden, near a tall fence that surrounded a small area behind the house. The place was neat, uncluttered, almost picturesque.

Leslie recognized the house from having seen it in all those pictures of Randy growing up. Although it could not really claim any definite architectural style that Leslie knew of, she felt certain it had been built in the late fifties or early sixties. The white-brick home, trimmed in a light shade of mint green, had the type of windows that had to be cranked to open, and there were two doors opening onto the front porch like so many homes built back then had. Also, she could tell by the height of the porch that the house had been built a few feet off the ground and not on a slab, as most brick homes were built today.

Leslie felt her heart pounding ferociously in her chest and adrenaline burning through her veins as she turned down the long, oil-topped drive. The moment she had been both longing for and dreading had arrived. Her anticipation—and apprehension—mounted until she thought she would explode. When she pulled around to the widened area of the driveway at the back of the house, she noticed Randy's coupe sitting right beside a bright-blue 1955 Chevy and a black 1984 Econoline van. She found a certain solace in seeing Randy's car and knowing he was nearby.

Parking directly behind Randy's coupe, Leslie took another quick glance around. There was a shiny brown Marquis parked inside the double garage, along with a dilapidated old pickup that was covered with so many different colors Leslie could not begin to guess which had been the original. One thing could be said for the old truck—it was unique. Other than what was in the garage, Leslie was not able to see much. Because of an eight-foot fence, Leslie could not even get a glimpse of the backyard.

"Well, do we walk around to the front door, go to that garage door there, or enter that opened gate?" Carol asked as she reached for the door handle.

"Don't ask me." Leslie shrugged and got out of the

car. She stalled for time by straightening her gray slacks and loose-fitting black blouse, hoping someone would step outside and greet them. "Where is Randy? Didn't he hear us drive up?"

"Obviously not," Carol said, looking around. When no one came out, she took the initiative and headed for the opened gate, with Leslie right behind her. Stepping inside the fence, they found a most unusual sight. There, lying belly down and propped up on bended elbows on the brick terrace was Randy, wearing faded jeans and a short-sleeved knit shirt, and to his left was a brown-haired, blue-eyed young woman, also in jeans and a casual cinnamon-colored blouse.

Lying in between the two adults was a small, lanky boy, six or seven years old, dressed in dark-blue coveralls. Sagging white socks with unmatched color bands were protruding from the pant legs, making one aware of the worn running shoes that had been left untied. The three of them were deep in concentration over an intense game of pick-up sticks.

Randy was first to look up and notice them. He grinned sheepishly, realizing how ridiculous he must look to them. Quickly, he got to his feet, brushed himself off, and began the introductions.

"Leslie, Carol, I want you to meet my kid sister, Jean. You've got to watch out for her—she's one mean pick-up sticks player. The only one who can beat her is her son, Curt, the little guy beside her with most of the pick-up sticks in his pile. He's the champ around here."

"Hi." The lovely young woman looked up and smiled at them. "Mind if I don't get up? I might get a turn at this yet. That is, if he'll ever make a mistake and give me a sporting chance."

The little boy waited until he had effortlessly lifted a sliver of yellow from the colorful tangle of plastic sticks scattered on the brick floor before he glanced around. Adding the yellow piece to his pile, he asked, "Either of you got kids?"

When Leslie admitted that they did not, he returned his attention to the game, effectively dismissing the new arrivals.

Being too far behind to have any hopes of winning, Randy wished his sister luck and led Leslie and Carol up the back steps and through a sliding glass door. They passed through a room that looked as if it had at one time been the back porch but had been glassed in and made into a lovely solarium. The room was rich in greenery.

Next they were led into the kitchen, where Leslie immediately recognized the woman peeking under the lid of a huge steaming pot as Randy's mother. She looked just like her pictures. She was not very tall, about five feet six, with short white hair that had either been permed or was naturally very curly. The stark white of her hair contrasted with the brown of her enormous eyes. Leslie wondered how Randy's eyes had come out such an uncanny shade of blue when his mother's were as dark as her own. The woman looked up, spotted the new guests, and rushed toward them, wiping her hands on her apron as she went.

"Glad you could come. I'm Lil," she said, greeting them both warmly. "Now which one of you is Leslie? No, let me guess. You are." She reached for Leslie's hand and held it a moment before releasing it. "When Randy finally got around to finding himself a girl, he did a good job of it. You're very lovely."

Leslie felt herself blushing at the woman's close scrutiny. Not knowing exactly how to respond, she simply sputtered a brief "Thank you."

"And you must be the friend she brought for protection," the woman went on to say, offering her hand to Carol.

"You got that one right!" Carol chuckled at the woman's perception. "Leslie's scared to death to be meeting you."

"Carol!" Sometimes Carol's blatant honesty made Leslie want to strangle her. She considered taking the sash of Carol's burnt-orange jumpsuit and wrapping it securely around her friend's big mouth.

Nodding, the woman's smile deepened, and Leslie could see where Randy had gotten his long dimples. "I don't blame her. We Brinnads are an awful lot. Randy, why don't you take her on into the den and introduce her to everyone? I need to check on supper."

Randy was amused by Leslie's discomfort, and his eyes sparkled as he led them through the corner of a long hallway into a large room where several people were crowded around the television watching a football game. One at a time, Leslie and Carol were introduced to the members of the group, starting with Randy's father, Harrison, a cheerful man, sixtyish, with thinning gray hair and sky-blue eyes. This was where Randy's eyes had come from. They even had the same devilish sparkle and thick fringe of lashes.

"So you're Leslie," the man commented, his eyes

narrowing as he appraised her. "Randy, I had no idea you had inherited my good taste in women." He smiled, then added with a sly wink, "Be sure you tell your mother what I just said. I can use all the Brownie points I can get right now. She's still mad about the ax handle I got her for Christmas."

Leslie wondered why a man would get his wife an ax handle for Christmas, but was afraid to ask. Strange thoughts drifted through her mind.

Sitting on the couch with Harrison was another gray-haired man, who looked to be about the same age. He was introduced as Harrison's older brother, Harold, and he, too, had wondrously blue eyes.

"Harry got her an ax handle to measure her backside with," Harold offered, realizing Leslie was curious about the gift. "Her father used to always tell her that when you got as broad as an ax handle, it was time to do something about it. Lil's always worried about her weight and going on diets even though she really doesn't need to, so Harrison decided to get her a measuring stick, the ax handle." Harold paused a moment, then, as if confiding in her, he added, "You must understand, my younger brother was not blessed with much common sense."

Although Randy's Uncle Harold did not really look very much like Harrison, Randy explained that the brothers were actually twins, and though Harold was older only by about forty minutes, he never would let anyone forget he was, indeed, the elder.

"Age before beauty," Harrison commented with an exaggerated wiggle of his eyebrows.

Harold responded with a playful growl.

Next Leslie and Carol were introduced to Jim Hawtly, thirtyish, who it turned out was Jean's husband and Curt's father. Leslie thought Jim looked remarkably like Conway Twitty, the country music star, but decided not to say so. With her luck, the man might not like Conway in the least and might take it as an offense.

Slumped in a chair next to Jim was a younger man, about Leslie's and Carol's age, frowning intently at the television, looking up only when Randy called his name. This was Tommy, the brother who had lost his wife almost two years before. He seemed more than a little depressed as Randy had said he would; he looked miserable.

"Hey, you look like you just lost a really big football bet. What's the matter? Your team letting you down?" Carol asked, taking an immediate interest in the young man, who merely nodded in response.

Leslie could easily see why Carol would be interested, even though she had failed to mention Tommy to her friend. Tommy was extremely good-looking, in spite of the hollow look on his face. He resembled Randy in many ways, only his features were slightly rounder and he looked as if he might be a little shorter. He had the same crystal eyes, and his nose looked exactly like his brother's. Leslie wondered if his smile would be as endearing.

"What game are you watching?" Carol asked, and not waiting for an invitation, she sat down in the chair closest to Tommy. Before anyone was able to answer, she recognized the uniforms of the two local teams and called out the names herself.

"You know much about football?" Tommy asked, glancing away from the set with interest.

"Enough," she replied. She did not mention that

she had been one of Leslie's best receivers when they were kids and had been able to outrun the fastest boy on the block. After all, she had quit trying to outrun boys years ago. "If they wouldn't keep changing the rules all the time, I'd know a lot more. About the time you get used to the game one way, they decide to change it."

Randy leaned toward Leslie and whispered, "If she really does know her football, those two are going to get along just fine. Tommy is a avid football fan."

"And what about you?"

"I'd much rather be playing it than watching it. Especially if there happens to be a sexy little quarterback to sack."

She was so tempted to ask if he happened to have a football handy, but managed to restrain herself. Yet her thoughts strayed in that direction several times after that.

For the next hour, they joined the others and watched the last half of the college game that had been in progress when they arrived. Harrison and his brother constantly argued over everything, from referee calls to which cheerleader had the greatest-looking legs. Although they kept raising their voices or slamming their beer mugs on the coffee table in front of them, they seemed to be enjoying every minute of it. Whenever one of them happened to ask Leslie for an opinion, she laughingly refused to mediate. Carol didn't have to refuse—she had a strange way of agreeing with both of them and getting away with it.

During the final quarter of the game, another couple joined the group. Harrison and Harold's younger sister,

Stella, and her husband, Jewell, were allowed to squeeze into the small vacant area on the couch.

When the game was over, Randy sighed wearily and suggested to Leslie that they go see if they could help his mother. When they passed through the hallway, Randy placed his arm possessively around Leslie's waist. Her own arm moved to his waist as if it belonged there.

"Mother, you need any help? Here're two ablebodied assistants, ready to work," Randy offered as they came to a stop just inside the door.

"No, I have things well in hand, but it would be nice if you two would stay in here and keep me company for a little while," she said, and looked up from the stove. Smiling, she did not miss the casual way their arms were around each other.

"I guess we can handle that," Randy said assuredly. Letting go of Leslie, he motioned toward the small table that stood nearby.

Moving the platter of sliced turkey closer to him, Randy began sampling some of the succulent smaller pieces, despite his mother's staunch warnings that he was going to ruin his appetite. Leslie couldn't help laughing at Randy, who, though he didn't stop nibbling at the tender pieces of meat, did have enough sense to flinch every time his mother came near.

With great effort, Lil ignored Randy and subtly began prying into Leslie's personal affairs as she went about getting the meal out into serving dishes. Without actually coming out and asking, she maneuvered the conversation in such a way that she got Leslie to admit that she had never been married, could cook a decent meal so long as she had a timer that functioned, would not be opposed to a large family, and even that she had never had a speeding ticket—which was pure luck, of course.

Leslie was not the only victim of Lil's subtle prying. She also managed to elicit information from Randy. Unaware, he admitted how much time he had been spending lately in pursuit of Leslie and how he had the same as proposed to her and even though she had not said yes, she also had not said no. Leslie, amazed at the woman's shrewdness, felt a strange sort of delight that she was as curious as she seemed to be about what was going on between them.

While Lil was still asking questions, Jean and Curt came in from outside. Plopping down in one of the kitchen chairs while Curt went on into the den to join the others, Jean asked with playful sarcasm, "Well, does Mother know your complete life history by now?"

"Sheryl Jean Brinnad Hawtly," Lil warned her daughter in a low, even voice.

"Ma'am?" When she saw the sweet expression of false innocence on Jean's face, Leslie recognized the strong resemblance between brother and sister.

"Put the ice in the glasses—supper's nearly ready," Lil said abruptly, clearly not what she had at first intended to say.

Slowly, Jean pulled herself out of the chair and went to the refrigerator to do as she was told. "Well, Mother, tell me—does she pass inspection?"

Lil lowered her lashes with a look of such murderous intent that Jean raised her hands as if surrendering. Then Lil nodded and, with a warm smile and a laugh, she said, "Actually, yes, she does pass. I like Leslie. She's going to make a fine daughter-in-law. I just wish I could have gotten the chance beforehand to decide on *you* for my daughter."

Randy laughed heartily at that remark, and Jean tossed a piece of ice haphazardly over her shoulder without so much as turning around and scored a direct hit. Wiping the moisture off his cheek, he laughed even harder.

This lighthearted family banter continued right through the meal, which lasted almost an hour. Once everyone's interest in the food had lulled, they all continued to sit around the table, nibbling at what was left on their plates and talking about whatever came to mind. Tommy and Carol seemed to be getting along very well. Leslie had finally been able to see that Tommy's smile indeed was very much like his brother's.

Leslie was not quite used to such a family atmosphere, having been brought up as an only child and having only one cousin living near enough to see often enough to know by name. She loved the warmth shared by everyone. She loved the interruptions, the arguments, and the different reactions to everything said. She was clearly being included as part of the family, and so was Carol. It was a nice feeling to be made a definite part of such a fun-loving group, but the nicest part of the evening was being with Randy. Often during the meal, she would glance over and catch Randy gazing intently at her. Whenever he knew he had her attention, he would give her a suggestive wink, and she couldn't help but smile in response.

After supper, everyone moved back to the den and settled into the comfortable furniture except Curt, who had disappeared as soon as he finished his second dessert. A peaceful aura settled over the group as the family leaned back and started to reminisce. Leslie listened eagerly to the stories, especially when they were about Randy's childhood. Some of the things Jean told about him made Dennis the Menace sound like a little angel in comparison.

"He accomplished quite a lot as a child," Jean said with a wry smile. "He's done a little of everything. I remember the time he fed my pet goldfish silver and gold glitter for supper. The next morning I found them floating belly up in their little bowl."

"Hey, I told you why I did that," Randy said in quick defense of himself. "I thought it would make them shine better." When everyone looked a little doubtful, he complained, "Hey, give me a break—I was only six years old at the time."

"And I suppose you're going to use the excuse of being only seven when you decided to tamper with the U.S. Postal System," Jean went on, eager to tell tales on her older brother. She turned directly to Leslie to explain. "Randy's always been thoughtful, as well as industrious. Having decided the postal system was totally unjust, dear little Randy set out to make things right. He followed the mailman around one day, gathering up all the mail just moments after it had been delivered until his little arms couldn't carry any more. Then he divided it in more equal amounts so that everyone got their share and redistributed it. Of course, it didn't dawn on him that the writing on the outside had anything to do with it."

"Yes, and it took me all day to straighten the mess out," Lil put in. "I can't remember how I found out about it, but I do remember how mad I was. Randy, do you remember how we found out about that particular escapade?"

"No, I don't remember how you found out exactly, but I do remember the *end* results," Randy said indignantly, reaching back and rubbing the area that had been most affected by his father's wrath.

"Seems most of your escapades had the same *end* result," Jean said, laughing. "Oh, I remember when you were so far ahead of your time that you took up streaking buck naked through the neighborhood even before it had become a national fad."

When Leslie raised her eyebrows, Randy quickly defended himself. "Hey, I got paid a quarter to do that."

"A quarter well spent," Leslie whispered so that only he could hear, and he responded with an unsettled smile.

Jean did not stop with tales of his childhood; she went on to his adolescent years and told how Randy had decided he was born to be a hippie. "His favorite words were, 'Peace and love, brother.'"

"Speaking of hippie," Randy said in a menacing tone, letting his gaze fall pointedly below her waist. When she realized that he was referring to the fact that her hips, though shapely, were perhaps a bit rounder than normal, she shook a fist in warning, and Randy reacted by holding his first two fingers up in the shape of a V and chanting, "Hey, peace and love, sister."

When it was time to leave, Leslie realized she was more fond of Randy than ever. She wished she could have known him when he was growing up but was glad that at least she knew him now. It occurred to her that she wanted him always to be a part of her life, that she wanted all these people to remain part of it. Maybe she *was* ready to commit herself to someone. This day had certainly brought her one step closer to knowing what was actually in her heart. Randy, seeming to sense her happy thoughts, had smiled knowingly at her all through the evening.

After Carol and Leslie had said their final good-byes, Tommy and Randy walked with them outside to Leslie's car. While Tommy followed Carol to the passenger side, where they said their own, timid good-byes, Randy joined Leslie at the driver's door. Everyone had seemed reluctant for them to leave and Leslie herself would have loved the day to go on forever.

"Thanks for coming," Randy said, stepping nearer in the darkness.

"Thank you for inviting me." She smiled, then shivered. Although the temperature had nearly reached the seventies that afternoon, it had now dropped, and the air was chilly.

"Mind if I kiss you?" he asked, taking her hands in his and rubbing them to warm them. Her fingers became alive with sensations.

"I'd mind if you didn't," she admitted, not bothering to suppress her smile.

"Is that so?" he asked with interest.

"That's so."

Enveloping her in his strong arms, he pressed his lips

to hers in a gentle, sweet, caring kiss. Suddenly the chill of the night air was gone, and all Leslie was aware of was the encompassing warmth of his body. The kiss did not last as long as Leslie would have wanted, but it was enough to stay with her for the rest of the night.

"See you tomorrow," he promised before letting go.

It took all the might Leslie had to turn and get in the car, and as they drove away, both she and Carol felt as though they had left something special behind. There was an unspoken agreement to silence between them as they headed back to Shreveport. Each wanted a quiet time to dwell on her personal thoughts and feelings. It had been quite a day.

Chapter Eight

Leslie did not know what time to expect Randy, only that he intended to stop by and pick up the tool chest sometime after he returned from Marshall. She did not even know if he planned to come by her place first or wait until he had been to his house. His tendency to do the unexpected forced Leslie out of bed early in order to clean and straighten the apartment. Although Sunday was her only day off, except for certain holidays like yesterday, and she usually spent the first half of those precious Sundays in bed either snoozing or reading the Sunday newspaper, today she was "up and at 'em" shortly after seven.

By ten o'clock, Leslie not only had the apartment gleaming once again, she had gotten dressed in a cuddly, warm blue velour jogging outfit and had put on her makeup just so. She had also brushed her hair to as close to perfection as possible. Glancing at her watch, she wished she had come right out and asked Randy what time he thought he would be coming by. If he was planning to stay most of the day in Marshall and not come home until that evening, she had a long, lonesome wait ahead of her.

Turning her attention to the newspaper, Leslie scanned the articles that interested her, often letting her mind drift off to thoughts of Randy instead. More and more, she hated the times they were apart, and wished he would hurry. Finally, just after noon, there was a loud knock at her door.

"Thank goodness," she said aloud, and quickly gathered up the newspaper sections. Not wanting to take the time to dispose of them properly, she shoved them under the skirt of a large upholstered chair near the front door. On her way to the door, she checked her reflection in a wall mirror, wanting to be sure she looked her best.

"Coming," she called out, then arranged her features in what she felt was an extremely sultry expression, very much like the one the heroines used in those very old movies that could be seen on the local channels late at night, Leslie, reaching the door, slowly let it swing open. Draping her form against the doorframe, she purred, "Welcome to my humble abode."

Lifting an eyebrow, Carol paused before saying anything. "Thanks. I appreciate it."

Raising her lowered lashes to find Carol mocking her with a silly "I didn't know you cared" expression on her face, Leslie stepped back and snapped, "Oh, get in here."

"Were you by chance expecting someone else?"

"Possibly," Leslie admitted, pursing her lips in exasperation. "What are you doing here?"

"Is that any way to greet your very best friend?"

"No," Leslie admitted with a smile, knowing that
Carol was indeed her very best friend and also that her
visit would help the time pass until Randy finally arrived.

As soon as Carol had helped herself to a diet cola and
joined Leslie on the couch, she dove headfirst into a
conversation about their visit to Marshall. The more
she talked, the more Leslie realized that Carol was
quite smitten by Randy's younger brother. It was
Tommy this and Tommy that. Leslie finally got up the
courage to ask, knowing Carol certainly would demand
to know if the situation was reversed, "Just how much
do you like this guy?"

"A lot. He's so sensitive and thoughtful. And
smart."

Carol's words surprised Leslie. Usually the first nice
things Carol had to say about a guy related to his good
looks or fantastic body, but this time she had noted the
deeper, finer qualities first.

"Well, you certainly seemed to bring him out of his
dour mood yesterday," Leslie observed, then watched
as Carol's eyes glittered with excitement.

"Do you really think so? I hoped I made a good impression. I was worried I might not have—you know
how I have a slight tendency to come on a little too
strong."

"Slight?"

"Well, I must have done something right, or he
wouldn't have agreed to come to Shreveport next
weekend and take me out to see that new play at the
Gaslight."

Leslie frowned. "You didn't tell me anything about that." But then they had said very little about anything last night on the way back.

Carol shrugged and said, "So, I'm telling you now."

Hours passed, and the conversation kept straying back to Carol's favorite new topic, Tommy. It was nearly four o'clock before Carol mentioned leaving for the first time. With Carol it always took at least three announcements before she actually left. She always found something else to mention before going, which usually led to another thing she almost forgot, which always reminded her of one thing more she should say.

Leslie and Carol were standing just inside the front door when another loud knock sounded. Leslie did not have to move to open it. She just reached for the knob and swung the door open.

"That was quick. You must have really been anxious to see me," Randy taunted as he stepped inside and planted an undemanding kiss on her forehead. "I must finally be getting to you—now if I could only get *at* you." A lecherous gleam filled his crystal eyes. Then, noticing Carol's interested expression, he nodded politely in her direction and winked.

Wincing when Leslie slammed the door behind him in a most meaningful manner, he waited for her impending tirade, but she amazed him with her mellow invitation to come in and sit down. "Unless you're in a hurry to get home."

"No, I've got the rest of the afternoon to impose," he informed her, then headed automatically for the refrigerator to see what she had in the way of liquid refreshment. Finding a cold beer, he helped himself.

"Hey, Carol, you certainly made quite an impression on my kid brother," he said as he sank down into his favorite corner of the couch.

"Did I?" Carol asked, eager to hear more.

"Hmm, and I see he made quite an impression on you."

Carol actually blushed. Leslie, who could not remember anything ever having had that effect on her friend before, stared in astonishment at the deep color in Carol's cheeks.

"Tommy hasn't considered taking anyone out for any reason since Kim died. Last night, he told me all about your plans to go see a play next weekend. He seems more like his old self again. I had planned to thank you for being so kind, but I see kindness had nothing to do with it. By the way, he intends to call you this evening with the excuse of having to change the time of your date."

"He does? He plans to call today? I'd better go get ready," Carol said excitedly, and turned to leave.

"For a phone call?" Leslie wondered aloud.

Turning to see the teasing glint in Leslie's eyes, Carol lowered her lashes in warning as she reached for the knob. "Oh, shut up."

Leslie couldn't help laughing.

After Carol had left, Randy patted the couch next to him in an attempt to get Leslie to sit down beside him.

"Seems both of the Brinnad boys have fallen madly in love," he observed with a contented smile. "And Mother is beside herself with joy. She's already planning what to wear to both weddings."

"Weddings?"

"Oh, yes. She's making her plans early. By the way, although she does believe that our wedding should be first since I'm the oldest, she wants us at least to wait until April. She loves the thought of a wedding in the springtime when the trees are full again and the air is alive with the sweet fragrance of flowers. Those are her words, not mine. It doesn't really matter to her if it's a church wedding or not, although she did hint that it would be nice. She knows your mother is supposed to get to make all the plans, but she really hopes you will let her be a part of it all. She really enjoyed putting Jean's wedding together. She's a real sentimentalist."

"Wait a minute. Why is she so sure there's going to be a wedding?"

"Because she knows I want a wedding. I realize the modern thing is to live together for a while, but I would rather go ahead and get married first. You know me and my commitments. And I'm rather partial to a church wedding myself."

"I thought you were going to give me more time. Why are you suddenly pushing for a wedding?" Leslie wasn't sure why, but she realized she was getting very angry over the prospect that he seemed so sure of himself and was making plans that included her when he had no real right to do so.

"Mother's eagerness rubbed off on me." He shrugged, reaching for her in a playful effort to take her in his arms. When she jerked free of his grasp and got up from the couch to pace about the room, he, too, started to get angry. "Look, I've let you know from the start what my intentions are."

"And I've let you know mine, too," she said angrily.

She knew she was overreacting but could not seem to stop herself. "I told you how I felt about the confinements of marriage, how I was opposed to being anyone's personal property, and here you are making your plans to bind me to you forever. Look, I'll make my own plans for my own future, thank you."

"But I told you all along marriage is what I wanted," he retorted, his voice rising.

"And what about what I want?"

"I honestly thought you were coming to terms with this ridiculous phobia of yours. Being the fool that I am, I actually thought you were finally falling in love with me and would want to be my wife. Yesterday was so nice—you seemed different, and we were getting along so well. I thought you were really enjoying yourself. You seemed to have liked being with me, and I thought I saw something new and special in the way you were looking at me. I guess I read you all wrong."

"Just because I enjoy your company doesn't mean I want to marry you. I used to enjoy John's company, but I never chose to marry the man." Her voice had climbed so high that she was straining to get the words out. "I'm sorry you see my reluctance to be tied down for the rest of my life as a ridiculous phobia, but that's the way it is. Besides, I enjoy my life just as it is."

"Looks like I did read you all wrong," he growled, then rose and headed for the door.

"Where are you going?"

"The hell away from here."

"What about your tool chest?"

"Mail it to me!"

Moments later he was gone.

Stunned by what had just happened, Leslie slowly sat down on the couch right next to where Randy had just been sitting. His body warmth was still there. Her anger melted into misery. What had come over her? She had acted like a shrew. What was it about the word "marriage" that scared her so?

Maybe Randy had been right, and it was some sort of a phobia. If that was so, maybe it could be dealt with. He had been right about yesterday. She *had* begun to feel differently about the idea of spending the rest of her life with him, and obviously the difference had shown. Why shouldn't he have hoped for the best?

"What's wrong with me?" she cried out. Tears slipped effortlessly down her cheeks as she realized how much she had overreacted. Her rage had been uncalled for. He had not done anything so terrible. What had triggered her? Now that he was gone, it seemed unreasonable that the mere fact that he had assumed she was ready to get married had caused such a drastic reaction.

Knowing full well that Randy deserved an apology, Leslie wiped the tears from her face with the soft sleeve of her shirt and went in search of a tissue. She would calm down, and once she had her emotions in check, she would call him. Better yet, she would touch up her makeup and drive over to his house and try to talk this out in person.

Only minutes later, Leslie had done what repairs she could to her makeup. She wished her eyes hadn't been still slightly swollen, but she didn't want to wait until they appeared normal. She was suffering from the agony of knowing she had ruthlessly hurt Randy when he had not really deserved it. She had to ease this pain inside her by getting things straight between them as soon as possible. With determined hope, she grabbed her keys and rushed to her car.

When she neared his house, she noticed that his car was not out front. Just in case he had somehow managed to squeeze it into that crowded garage of his, she stopped and knocked lightly on the door.

"Randy," she called out as she tried the doorbell. There was no answer. Discouraged, she sank down and sat on the only doorstep. She would wait for his return. Glancing at her watch and seeing that it was almost five-thirty, she knew it would be getting dark soon and the temperature would start dropping rapidly.

When darkness set in and Randy had not shown up yet, Leslie decided to risk his having her arrested and tried the doorknob. As she expected, the door was locked. So were the garage doors and the back door. She even tried the only two windows that were not guarded by huge, threatening holly bushes, and they were latched shut. Not wanting to set her posterior back down on that cold cement and seeing nothing to provide her a more comfortable place to sit, Leslie went to wait in the car.

With the heater for company, Leslie was able to prolong her vigil several more hours before deciding to give it up. She could not imagine where he might have gone. She wondered where she would have gone if she had been in his place and realized she either would have wanted to find a quiet spot where she could be alone to sort out her feelings or else would have headed up to Carol's to get a friend's viewpoint.

For some reason Leslie could not remember the names of Randy's closest friends, never having had the opportunity to meet them, and would not have known where they lived even if she could remember the names. Finally, she decided to go back to her apartment and try calling every half hour or so until he came home.

Once back in her apartment, Leslie crawled into bed with a book she'd been wanting to read, and she made periodic calls to Randy's house. She dialed his number every twenty to thirty minutes until just after eleven-thirty, when sleep overcame her.

The next morning when she awoke, she realized she had failed to set the alarm and was running late. She knew Randy would already be at her mother's, so she decided not to phone but wait until she could get over there and talk to him face to face.

To her dismay, when she did finally arrive at her mother's, Randy's car was not in the drive. Thoughts of his having quit, or worse, having been in an accident of some sort, nagged at her as she entered through the kitchen.

"Mom?" she called out as she made her way through the house.

"In here" came the distant reply.

She found her mother in the dining room, munching on a piece of overdone toast and finishing off half a grapefruit.

"Mom, where's Randy? His car isn't outside."

Never one to talk with her mouth full, Margaret shrugged and motioned to her water glass, letting her daughter know it would be a moment before she replied. Leslie waited impatiently.

"He called a while ago and said that he would be late. He's stuck in Marshall with a bad water pump, and he won't be able to get a new one until the stores open. He said it would only take half an hour to put in a new pump once he has one, and he'll be here sometime this morning."

Leslie felt such relief. He was safe and had not gotten so angry that he quit. Although she wondered why he was back in Marshall, she could at least stop worrying about him for now. She would plan to have that talk wih him during her lunch break.

The morning passed with incredible slowness, despite the problems that usually came right after Christmas. Lovall's always had many complaints in those first few days after the holidays, when everyone brought things back that they did not like or could not fit into. Leslie tried to remain placid while rotund ladies argued indignantly that the clothes they received were obviously sized wrong. Men were eager to exchange their new multicolored ties for anything with a bit of taste, while teenagers swarmed the counter, eager to swap the less than "cool" albums they had received for Michael Jackson's latest release. Everyone had a complaint, whether directed at Lovall's or at the idiot who had purchased the gift. By lunchtime, Leslie was more than eager to get away and have her talk with Randy.

Just before it was time to leave, Margaret called. "Leslie, I won't be able to go home with you to eat lunch. A friend of mine has stopped in and wants me to go out to eat. I'll just have my friend drop me off at the house later. Is that all right with you?"

"Of course, Mother. Enjoy yourself."

Leslie was delighted at the news. She would not have to wait until they were through eating to have a private talk with Randy. She could apologize immediately and get the air cleared between them right away.

The sooner the better.

Eagerly, she hurried over to her mother's. She was very glad to see his coupe sitting in the driveway. Rushing inside, she was not prepared for the cold reception she got. Randy seemed stiff and his manner stilted when she entered the kitchen, and after she greeted him with a tentative hello, he turned and glowered at her. She stared at him in stunned silence. She did not have to ask—it was plain to see that he was still very angry at her.

"I, uh, I see you managed to get your water pump fixed," she stammered. Mentally, she cowered beneath the harsh stare.

"Your lunch is ready. Shall I serve now?"

"Not yet. I have something I want to talk to you about."

"You don't have to bother. I already know all about it."

"You do?" she asked cautiously. Then why was he still so angry?

"Yes, I was here when they called, and not knowing anything about it, I asked to take a message."

"Who called?" Leslie could not see a trace of logic in what he was saying. She had not told anyone about their argument.

"Creel's Housekeeping," he said between clenched teeth.

"Creel's Housekeeping?" Now why did that sound

familiar? Then it dawned on her why. "Creel's House-keeping called?"

"Yes, they called wanting to speak to either you or your mother. As is my custom, I asked to take a message." Reaching into his shirt pocket, he pulled out a piece of folded paper and thrust it at her. "They called to tell you that they did indeed have a full-time person available, and if you wanted, the woman could come by and speak with you at your convenience. She can start as early as next Monday. They want you to call and talk to them about it as soon as possible. The number is on that paper, although I'm sure you have it committed to memory."

Leslie accepted the paper and stared at it in horror.

"I guess I should have expected an underhanded trick like this," he continued, "but it honestly took me by complete surprise. Just because you were afraid I was trying to pressure you into something you don't want, you decided to go behind my back and have me replaced. I never would have thought you could be this spiteful." Randy's gaze turned the color of blue steel, and his jaw looked rock-hard.

Leslie felt as if her insides were collapsing. Her mind tried to convince her that this wasn't happening, but the fierce pounding in her heart told her that indeed it was.

"Look, Leslie, I happen to enjoy working for your mother," he went on, "and I particularly like taking care of this beautiful old house. Just because you're afraid I'm going to tread on your precious independence and cause you to do something against your will, you don't have to have me fired. Although I admit it will be hard as hell, I can actually manage to control myself where we are concerned.''

He paused, giving her a chance to speak. When she did not respond, he said, ''I'm well aware of the rules you like to run your relationships by, and I can well abide by them. You want a platonic relationship—well, so be it. Hard as it will be, I can even keep my hands to myself. I promise. No more touching and trying to make you fall in love with me. Just don't have me fired. I love this job, and I really can't bear the thought of never seeing you again. Please, Leslie, have a heart. You do have a heart, don't you?''

That remark hurt. Closing her eyes to the confusion and pain, Leslie realized that the call from Creel's could not have been timed any worse. After her tirade the day before, he was justified in believing the worst. Why hadn't she had the good sense to call Creel's back and cancel? Once she had quit wanting to get Randy out of her life, she had never given a second thought to that call she had made what seemed now so long ago, but it all came screaming back to her now. She had asked Creel's to let her know as soon as they had a full-time prospect, and her intent then had indeed been to have Randy replaced. But that had been before she had gotten to know him, before she had become so fond of him. Damn her own stupidity!

''Randy, I didn't...'' She paused. How should she go about explaining this?

''Sorry, it won't work,'' he growled, his eyes cold with anger. ''The woman that phoned specifically mentioned that you were the one who had made the call.''

''Randy, let me explain.''

"Look, I don't want any explanations. Just don't have me fired out of spite. I want to keep this job. And I certainly won't try to pressure you with the idea of marriage anymore, and I won't try to get intimate, and I will finally accept the fact that you don't want a relationship with any strings whatsoever. I won't like it, but I can live with it."

Heaving a sarcastic breath, he added, "Rest assured—from now on any relationship between us will be strictly a platonic one, because I don't want anything in between. I know now that I can't have all of you and I never will. You don't love me. Christmas Day, I thought you did, but it was some sort of strange imitation, and I don't want to settle for an imitation. So a platonic relationship is actually the logical solution. How about it? Can we still be friends? Will you stop trying to have me fired?"

When Leslie did not reply immediately, he lowered his lashes as he told her, "Even if you do still plan to get your mother to fire me, I'll fight it. I not only like this job, I'm good at it, too. And if I have to, I'll explain the whole situation to her so she can make a fair decision. Your mother is the type who listens to reason. Consider that while you make your decision."

"Are you threatening me?"

"No, simply letting you know my intentions so you can make an intelligent decision—if that's at all possible."

"Randy, I want you to stay."

"Good, it's settled, then. I'll serve lunch now."

"I don't want lunch now." She wanted to explain how that call to Creel's had had nothing to do with their argument. She wanted him to know she had made that call the very first day she met him and had foolishly forgotten about it.

"Suit yourself," he said, then turned and walked abruptly from the room.

"Randy," she called after him. When he made no response, she went after him. "Randy, will you let me explain?"

"I already told you I don't need your explanations." She heard his voice coming from the laundry room. "It's settled. Just let it alone."

Leslie stood in the narrow hallway that joined the laundry room to the kitchen, wondering what she should do. Should she go in there and demand he listen? Would the fact that the call had been made weeks ago matter so much? After all, she had had every intention of having him replaced. He could not be too pleased with the idea, no matter when it had occurred. And he was sure to point out that all she had to do was to make one simple phone call to cancel her original request. Would it be better to wait until he was in a more receptive mood? He definitely did not want to discuss it now.

She tried one more time. "Randy?"

"I've got work to do," he shouted back.

No, he clearly did not want to talk about it now. At least she no longer had to worry about his constant attempts to make her want to be committed to him, to marry him. That was certainly a relief—or was it? The more she thought about it, the more complicated it all seemed to become. Tired from all the conflicting emotions, Leslie slowly turned and walked back into the kitchen. She would wait until Randy was interested in listening to her. At the moment he was too dead set against it.

Fighting tears as she went, Leslie returned to her office to try to bury her thoughts in her work. She did not dare return to the "Complaints and Returns" service desk. The way she felt right now she just might try to stuff the next fat lady into that size-eight dress and shove her out the door in it. It would be better for business to allow Cassie to help make the decisions as to what could and couldn't be returned.

As soon as Cassie returned from lunch, Leslie sent her downstairs, then closed her office door, called up Creel's to cancel her request for the housekeeper and then tried to lose herself in her work.

It didn't work. Leslie was not able to forget the hurt and anger in Randy's eyes, and as the day wore on, she wished she had gone ahead and tried to explain what had actually happened. So she would have had to admit that she really did at one time want him kicked out, but surely he could understand that she had not exactly been delighted with her first impression of him. Even if it did somehow make matters worse between them— which seemed next to impossible at the moment—at least she would have tried.

By five-thirty, when she was gathering together her sweater and purse, she had made up her mind to go over to Randy's and see if he would at least listen to her now.

When she pulled into his driveway, he was just getting out of his car. As he made his way around the front of the car to the passenger's side, he glanced back to see who was driving up and was clearly surprised to see her. Through the tiny oval rear window of the coupe, Leslie could see that Joey and his dog Barky were in the car.

"This is certainly a surprise," Randy commented coolly, letting his hand rest on the door handle.

"I was hoping we could have a talk. I had no idea you had company. I guess it can wait a little longer. I'll call you later."

"No, it's been bugging me all day that you had something to say and I refused to hear it. Joey won't mind. Grab a sack and come in," he said, opening the door and waiting until Joey and his shaggy little dog had bounded out of the car.

"Hi, Miss Leslie," Joey called before turning to grab one of the many sacks packed into the small confines of the car. "I get to help Mr. Randy fix supper, then him and me are going to play Monster Invaders on his television," the boy tossed over his shoulder as he tried to step around the eager dog bouncing wildly in front of him. "You gonna eat with us?"

Leslie paused. She certainly would have liked to, but the invitation really had to come from Randy.

"Sure she is," Randy chimed in as he gathered up three of the sacks. Stopping to give her a scolding look, he asked, "Well, aren't you going to help? There are still a couple of sacks in there."

"That's hard to imagine," she said, wondering how they had ever managed to get all those groceries into that tiny two-seater car.

As they carried the groceries into the kitchen, Randy, knowing Leslie's curiosity was aroused, went on to explain why Joey was with him. "Boy, did I luck out. On the day I had all this shopping to do and would have had to unload it all by myself, Joey's grandmother had an emergency come up. She asked your mother if she could watch Joey for a few hours, but your mother had plans of her own. That man she had lunch with also wanted to take her to dinner."

"That man?" Leslie asked. She had no idea her mother's luncheon friend had been a man. She wondered who it was.

"Yes, I forgot his name, but she said something about his being an old friend she hadn't seen in years."

Leslie could not imagine who the man was but knew she could find out all about him later. She listened as Randy continued his explanation.

"So, with only the most selfish of motives, I volunteered to have Joey come home with me." With an expression of exaggerated scheming on his handsome face, he looked toward Joey, who was busy pulling things out of sacks and scattering them across the kitchen table. "I knew I would be able to get lots of work out of him."

Joey grinned with pride, then set about putting the things away. Randy watched with an amused smile. Joey had his own ideas about where everything should go. When the boy placed the canned spinach in one of the bottommost drawers and covered it up with dish towels, Randy commented, "I have a feeling Joey doesn't want spinach for supper."

Seeing that Joey had the job well in hand, but still keeping an eye on where everything was going, Randy leaned against the countertop while he talked to Leslie.

"I must admit, I'm very surprised to see you here. I didn't know what limits you would set on a platonic relationship. I'm glad to know I can still invite you over for dinner now and again."

"I told you, I want to resolve the misunderstanding concerning Creel's."

"Misunderstanding?"

"Yes, there's something I want to explain that may make a difference. I'll admit that when I made that call to Creel's Housekeeping I indeed intended to convince Mom to replace you."

"That's really nice to know." Randy turned his face away for a moment, and when he finally turned to look at her again his facial muscles were taut and his eyes intense. "I'm so glad you came all the way over here to tell me that."

"Let me finish. I made that call the very same day you went to work for Mom. Right after you'd made all those cracks about me in that Santa suit and left the store. I was so angry I made the call thinking you were sure to blunder away the job anyway and I'd have another housekeeper all lined up. At that time, I was more than eager to see you go."

"You made the call way back then?" Randy's face relaxed as he listened, but he was still frowning.

"Yes, and once I changed my mind about you, I promptly forgot all about having made the call."

"What made you change your mind about me?" he asked eagerly. Now even the frown was gone. "Was it my uncanny charm or my virile good looks?"

"Well, it certainly wasn't your modesty," she said, pressing her lips together. "I'm sorry I didn't think to call them back and cancel, but I honestly forgot. I did call them this afternoon and explained that Mother was no longer needing new help."

Randy looked at her for a long time before finally speaking. "And I'm sorry that I blew up like I did. I'm really good at jumping to the wrong conclusion."

Leslie laughed, then looked down at her entwined fingers. "So where does all this leave us?"

"It looks as if we're still friends. I made that promise to abide by your rules, so I won't go back to pressuring you for a commitment you're not ready to make. From now on, it's hands off. We'll simply enjoy each other's company and see what happens. It's a heck of a lot better than not getting to be with you at all."

Leslie was not sure she liked the thought of her hands-off rule any longer. Although the rule had served a purpose in the past, she was not sure she still wanted it to be enforced. But for now, she knew it would help slow things down and give her more time to think her changing emotions through. She appreciated Randy's willingness to cooperate. It showed that he still cared.

"So, what's for supper?" she asked, ready to change the subject.

"Don't ask me. Ask the chef," Randy replied, pointing to Joey, who was busy stuffing a bag of flour into the bottom drawer of the stove. All the other drawers and cabinets at his level were already filled. "He's the one in charge tonight. I'm just the hired help."

Later, while the three of them dined on corndogs and ravioli, all the tension that had come between Randy and Leslie was gone. Although twice Randy had started to touch her for one reason or another, he remembered his promise and jerked his hand back before he actually did, muttering something under his breath about dumb rules.

After they ate, they went into the living room to play Monster Invaders, allowing Leslie to display her talent at shooting down space creatures. She ran up a score only Joey could seem to match.

"I hate this game," Randy complained to Leslie, disgusted with losing. "It's only that stupid promise not to touch you that's keeping me from grabbing you by that pretty throat of yours and squeezing until you turned a pleasing shade of blue."

Next, when Joey managed to beat him by more than twice his own score, he groaned aloud in his misery once more, "If only I wasn't so opposed to doing bodily harm to small children!" Glancing again at the final score, he wailed out his anguish and strangled a throw pillow instead.

Chapter Nine

"I'll wait here," Leslie told Randy as he got out of her car to go see if Joey was ready to leave.

Until Randy had called the night before to tell her that Joey was going with them, Leslie had hoped they were finally going to go somewhere alone, just the two of them. She had been looking forward to not having to share Randy with anyone else until they reached the picnic at his grandmother's and then again on the long drive home. So much for that.

It had not come as too much of a surprise when she learned they would again have someone else tagging along. For the past six weeks, every time they had plans to go anywhere, someone else had been invited to go along. Friday and Saturday night dates always included Tommy and Carol, which had been fine with Leslie at first, but recently she had found herself selfishly wanting to be alone with Randy. At least Carol got to be alone with Tommy on most Sundays. All of Leslie's Sunday outings with Randy had included either Tommy and Carol or her mother and Doyle, her newly reacquainted friend, or else Joey and Barky went along.

It was as though Randy no longer wanted to be alone with her, and she could certainly understand why. What point would there be for him to manage a moment alone with her when he felt he couldn't hold or touch her? Gritting her teeth against the misery of it all, she knew something had to be done about that foolish agreement between them. Her body ached with longing for him to touch her again.

Her rules had seemed just fine when she was seeing John, but John was no longer a part of her life—he'd finally given up ever finding her free anymore. She felt no remorse, only relief, over having lost John's interest. She wanted to spend all her free time with Randy, but, even more, she wanted to spend some of that time alone with him.

"Hi, Miss Leslie," Joey chirped as he opened the passenger door to her car and let Barky climb in first. Barky had been quick to learn that, although he could jump around Randy's coupe in wild abandon with no retribution to worry about, he was to sit still while on Leslie's velour seats. The decision to go in Leslie's car had come because they needed the trunk space. Randy was in charge of bringing hot dog and hamburger buns and had three large sacks full of both. Had he tried to fit them into the little turtle hull in the back of his car, they would surely have arrived with three crumpled heaps of bread crumbs. Going in her car had been the obvious solution.

"Hi, Joey," Leslie called back cheerfully. Despite her annoyance at not being able to be alone with Randy, she did not resent the little boy. It wasn't his fault Randy no longer wanted to be alone with her. Besides, who could resent such a sweet, smiling face, with its little pug nose spattered with adorable freckles?

"Hey, Joey, why don't you sit up front with us? There's plenty of room," Randy insisted, when Joey had pushed the back of the passenger seat forward in order to climb in beside Barky.

"If you're sure you don't mind," Joey replied slowly, looking to Leslie for reassurance.

"No, you're welcome to sit between us," Leslie said, letting out a weak sigh. "As long as you wear a seat belt."

Joey wasted no time climbing in front and digging out the center seat belt. He seemed to place some importance in sitting up front with the adults.

The two-hour drive over to Lake O' The Pines, where Randy's family was having its annual picnic to celebrate his grandmother's birthday, was pleasant. The sun was shining and the weatherman had promised temperatures in the upper seventies, which seemed strange when just a week earlier a brief three-inch snow had covered the ground during a spell of several days of freezing weather. But that was the way the weather was around that area—unpredictable.

Because of the remote area of the lake they were headed for, they turned off Interstate 20 at Marshall and headed north toward Jefferson. When they entered the small historic town that at one time had been a thriving river port on the Big Cypress Bayou, Randy wanted to know if either Leslie or Joey had ever been to one of Jefferson's annual pilgrimages.

"No, I haven't," Leslie answered. "But I've heard about them."

"I don't even know what one is," Joey admitted.

"Well, then, this May I'll have to bring you both to enjoy this very special event. Every year, Jefferson turns back the calendar, and many of the restored homes and buildings are opened to public tours. It's a real taste of the mid-1800s. I love to go to it."

Joey seemed very excited over the prospect, especially when he heard about the horse-pulled wagons and surrey rides. Leslie was not so sure she should allow Randy to make plans that far ahead. The way things had seemed to cool between them, she was not convinced they would still be seeing each other come May. She was not even certain they would make it through this short month of February. It was a depressing thought, but she felt it was an honest assessment of where their relationship seemed headed.

Randy went on to answer Joey's questions about what he could expect to find and do at the pilgrimage until they neared their destination, then Joey's questions took a turn to what he could expect to find and do at Randy's grandmother's. Leslie, too, was anxious to know what to expect, and she put aside her depressing thoughts to listen to Randy's description of the place. Following Randy's directions, given between answers to Joey's unending questions, Leslie had first turned down a curving, two-laned farm-to-market road, then she took the narrow tar-topped one-lane road that Randy had indicated. Finally she turned into a narrow graveled drive that was surrounded by thick woods.

"Spooky-looking," Joey noted. The driveway tunneled beneath the tall entwining branches of a variety of trees. Although many of them were live oak or pine and were still green and thick, several trees were bare, almost skeletal in appearance, with winter-gray vines draping the branches like eerie spiderwebs.

"You should see it at night," Randy commented ominously.

Joey frowned, remembering it was going to be night when they left. But just when it looked as though he was going to start complaining, they came upon a huge, sunny clearing with a large log house off to one side and a view of the lake several hundred yards beyond. With the sunlight dancing across the surface of the huge lake, it was much as Randy had described.

"What a neat place," Joey exclaimed as they drove closer.

"Yes, it is beautiful," Leslie quickly agreed as she took in her surroundings. There were dozens of cars parked haphazardly in front of the house and what appeared to both Leslie and Joey to be hordes of people milling about. Leslie was glad she had decided to wear jeans and a brightly colored western shirt instead of the slacks outfit she had started to put on. Everyone else was dressed extremely casually, most of them in jeans, too, including Randy, who looked exceedingly good in his tight denim pants. And he'd left his loose-fitting shirt unbuttoned at the top, exposing all that sexy chest hair.

Glancing around, Leslie was not surprised that Tommy's '55 Chevy was not among the parked cars. He and Carol were going to be late because Carol's family had had plans as well. When Leslie's widening gaze took in all the people, she hoped they wouldn't be too late. She needed Carol's sharp wit to hide behind. She could get dreadfully tongue-tied around strangers, while Carol was always at her best.

"Are all of these people relatives?" she wanted to know as she helped Randy get the sacks out of the trunk.

"Most of them. We use Grandma's birthday as an excuse to have a big reunion each year. Today you're going to be meeting my first cousins, second cousins and maybe even a few third cousins, as well as lots of aunts, uncles and great-aunts and so on. Some of them come every year, others come at least every other year. I told you it was a big family event."

Hugging a sack to her with no thought of what she was doing to the buns inside, she whispered softly, "But I had no idea you had so *much* family. When *we* have a family get-together, you can sit most of them at one long table."

He shrugged. "The Brinnads believe in large families." Then, looking at her, he added, "They also believe in round hamburgers. Here—give me that sack."

Before they managed to get three steps away from the car, they were greeted by the first of many unfamiliar faces. Leslie smiled when she was introduced, trying desperately to commit the new names to memory. But by the time she had been introduced to a dozen or so cousins, aunts and uncles, she had given up and hoped she could get by without knowing names. Minutes after they arrived, Joey was introduced to some other boys about his age, and they all went flocking down to the water's edge to see what wonderful treasures there were to be found.

"Do you think he'll be safe?" Leslie wanted to know

as she and Randy made their way through the throng of
friendly faces to the picnic area, where food was being
heaped onto picnic tables and cloth-covered camp
tables.

"When is a little boy as active as Joey ever safe?"
Randy wanted to know, giving her a "think about it"
grin. "He's safe enough. I know most of those boys—
they're good swimmers should he fall in."

"I guess I worry too much," she admitted and followed Randy on to the tables with no further comment.
Once relieved of his packages, Randy started to make
the rounds of his relatives, with Leslie trying to stay
right beside him. It would be hours yet before eating
time.

At some point late in the afternoon, Leslie made a
wrong turn or maybe didn't turn when she should
have, because when she looked back in the still-
growing crowd to say something to Randy, she discovered he wasn't there. She scanned the area quickly
but didn't find his face among the rest. People she had
been introduced to came up to see if she was enjoying
herself, while others were curious to find out who she
was. Occasionally her status was confused, and a few
relatives made it evident that they thought she was
Randy's wife. Avoiding lengthy explanations, she tried
to keep her conversations short so she could be free to
search for Randy. After greeting and being greeted by
many more strangers, she finally ran into Randy's
father. Relieved, she asked him if he had seen Randy.

"Last I saw of the boy, he was up at the house, out
on the lounging deck with Mother," he told her, mo-

tioning toward the top of the hill. "Now, tell me, have you seen Lil?"

"Sorry," she said, shrugging as she stood on tiptoe to peer toward the house. To her relief, she noticed Randy was still on the large wooden deck beside the house. "You're the first familiar face I've run into."

"Oh, well, I'll find her eventually," he said as he waved good-bye to her.

When she reached the deck, Leslie began threading her way through the people assembled there. Randy was standing next to two older women and had his arm draped casually around one, occasionally scanning the area as if he might be looking for her as well. Leslie easily guessed that the woman inside his casual embrace was the birthday girl, Randy's grandmother. Taking a deep breath, she stepped bravely forward for the impending introduction. She had been warned that his grandmother was not only very opinionated but rarely kept those opinions to herself—and the worst of it was, as Leslie had been told, the woman was usually right.

"Randy, I've been looking for you," Leslie began as she stepped around a small child who had stopped suddenly in her path. Randy had looked up, noticing her just before she spoke.

"I've been right here," he said; then, extending his free arm toward her, he added, "Come on over here—I want you to meet Grandma. Her name is Janna, but you can just call her Grandma; everyone does."

Leslie eagerly headed for his outstretched arm, wanting desperately for him to drape it over her shoulders in careless abandon the way he was doing to his grand-

mother, but just as she neared him, it was as though he
suddenly remembered his agreement not to touch her,
because he quickly jerked the arm back and let his hand
go instead to the pocket of his jeans. Leslie noticed his
grandmother's curious glance at such behavior.

"I've heard a lot about you," Leslie stammered,
feeling more and more uncomfortable as she noticed
the frown that had set into his grandmother's forehead,
drawing her deep wrinkles to a point.

"And I've heard a lot about you, dear," the woman
replied, slowly. "But I wonder."

Leslie knew that was an invitation from Randy's
grandmother to ask just what it was she had heard, but
she was not sure she wanted to know. Janna looked
wise with her years, and for some reason Leslie was
afraid of that. She searched her mind for something to
say that would change the subject without seeming too
abrupt. She did not want the woman to guess that she
was intentionally avoiding a conversation centered on
herself.

"Grandma and I were just catching up on what's
new. Since she went to Auny Amy's house for Christmas I didn't get to see her. I guess I haven't seen her
since last September," Randy said, sounding apolo-
getic.

"You'd think he'd at least come to do a little fish-
ing," Janna complained good-naturedly.

"Randy tells me you live out here all alone," Leslie
said, in hopes of keeping the conversation away from
anything that could affect her personally.

"Oh, it isn't so lonely. Between my grandchildren
and great-grandchildren, there's usually someone visit-

ing. Not all my grandsons ignore me like this one does."

"Grandma..." Randy moaned at the verbal shot his grandmother had just given him. But before he could comment further, they were interrupted by a frantic Barky. The shaggy little dog was jumping on Randy's leg and barking incessantly.

"What in the world?" Randy commented curiously.

Knowing Barky was never very far away from Joey, Leslie glanced around to see just where the child was. Finally, she spotted him working his way through the crowd. Huge tears were streaming down his face, and he was holding his arm out at an odd angle. She immediately noticed a trail of bright-red blood starting at his elbow and running all the way down his arm. Instantly Leslie ran toward the boy, arriving only seconds before Randy.

"Joey, what happened?" she asked, kneeling down to examine the wounded elbow.

"I fell on some rocks by the water," he said, sobbing, then catching a glimpse of the blood again, he started to cry harder.

"What were you doing on the rocks?" Randy asked, looking down over Leslie's shoulder at the still-bleeding wound.

"There was this turtle..." he started, but his words trailed off to nothing as they became lost in his wails of anguish.

"Enough said," Randy commented, knowing what a prize a turtle could be to a little boy.

"Let's get you into the house and see if we can't get that cleaned up and bandaged," Leslie said, lifting him up and carrying him the rest of the way. Randy's grandmother was already holding the door open when they reached the house and quickly escorted her to the main bathroom, where Leslie could find whatever first-aid materials she would need. Because the bathroom was small, Randy let the two women tend to Joey and stayed out in the wood-planked hallway until they were finished. Having seen that the elbow was just badly scraped, he knew the best thing for Joey was the tender loving care that women were so good at administering.

Taking a cotton ball soaked in the antiseptic Randy's grandmother had promptly provided, Leslie knelt down beside Joey and gently cleansed the raw area. As he watched her dab the blood away, Joey's wails were reduced to mild sobs.

"It doesn't look so bad now that I've cleaned away all that blood, now, does it?"

"N-no," he said, sniffing, as he gazed appreciatively into her eyes. His lips were still twisted into a pensive pout, but he had stopped crying.

"And once I get a Band-Aid on there, it will be almost as good as new, don't you think?"

"I guess s-so."

He watched silently as she removed the backing and eased the small bandage over his injury.

"There, all done." She smiled, giving the wounded elbow a light kiss for good measure, and watched the tension ease from his face.

"Thank you." He beamed, then wrapped his arms around her neck and gave her a huge hug.

"That's some little boy you have there," Randy's grandmother commented with a smile.

"Oh, he's some little boy, all right, but he's not mine," she explained while holding Joey tight.

"But, I...he seems...you..." Janna was clearly confused.

"He's just a good friend, aren't you, Joey?" When the boy nodded his head vigorously, she went on to say, "I wish I had a litle boy like Joey. When and if I ever do have children, I hope the first one's a boy and he's a lot like this little guy." Silently, she noted how lucky Joey's mother was to have such a sweet, loving little boy. She wondered how the woman could stand to spend so much time away from him. How could she put her career so far ahead of something so dear?

A deep, sinking feeling overwhelmed Leslie as it occurred to her that her own determination to put her career and her personal freedom first was keeping her from having children. In actuality, she was no different from the woman she had just scorned. Suddenly, her career did not seem so important, and her freedom made her feel desolate and terribly alone.

Leslie's maternal instincts had surfaced, and it suddenly occurred to her just what she was missing by living with her stupid fear of getting involved with what she had always considered the weaker, more confining emotions. She felt an empty ache. By denying her love and avoiding all thoughts of marriage and commitment, she was depriving herself of so much. It all seemed senseless now.

When she glanced up at Randy's grandmother, her newfound insights must have been evident, because the woman was staring at her as if she might possibly be going mad. With this sudden understanding of herself,

Leslie was eager to be alone to think things through, to view them in this new light. At the same time, she wanted to be able to tell Randy about what was happening to her. So unexpectedly, things seemed to be falling into place. She needed to be alone with him so they could talk, explore what her new feelings could mean to them both, but that was impossible at the moment.

A talk with Randy would have to wait until after they had taken Joey home. She was not going to drive Randy home as planned unless he agreed to invite her in for a while. She would take him captive if she had to, but they were going to have a talk—alone. He had to know that everything was different now. She was finally willing to face her truer feelings, and she was astounded at how sudden the revelation had been.

"Yes, I really would love to have a little boy like this," she marveled aloud, more to herself than to Randy's grandmother. *And maybe a little girl or two to keep him company,* she thought with a half smile. *All with uncanny blue eyes.*

When the three of them emerged from the bathroom, Randy pushed himself away from the wall where he had been leaning and went to inspect Joey's small bandage.

"Think you're going to live?" he wanted to know.

"Looks like it." Joey grinned; then, turning to Leslie, he asked, "May I go back outside now?"

"Sure, go ahead—just be careful," she warned him, realizing how much like a mother she sounded.

There was a new sparkle in Leslie's eyes when she looked at Randy that he couldn't help but notice. He stared at her a moment as if wondering what had gone on in that bathroom, then suggested they go back out and join the others. Several times after that, when they were visiting with different relatives, he caught her watching him with that same odd glint in her eyes. He would stare at her curiously, as if trying to fathom what was going on inside her strange little mind. She was aware that she was making him nervous, and realizing the tables had turned, she enjoyed every minute of it.

Finally it was time to eat, and after Leslie and Randy located Joey, the three of them got in line with all the others to fill their paper plates with burgers, hot dogs, baked beans, corn on the cob and assorted chips. Balancing their plates with one hand and carrying their iced tea with the other, they located a grassy spot and sat cross-legged on the ground.

"Doesn't it all look good?" Leslie asked, positioning her tall plastic cup in the grass so it would not easily spill. She was starving.

"And it smells so good," Joey added, taking a big whiff of the mounds of food on his plate.

"Let's see if it tastes as good." As soon as Leslie had helped Joey place his cup in a safe spot, she lifted her burger, stacked high with fresh vegetables, and took a huge, unladylike bite. Her appetite was voracious.

"What's gotten into you?" Randy asked, temporarily ignoring his own plate. "You seem different. I can't put my finger on it, but you suddenly seem giddy, like a bird in flight."

A bird in flight. That described the way her heart felt, all right. She could not help smiling.

"There you go again, smiling like some kind of nut," he pointed out. "What's with you?"

"I'll tell you all about it later," she said, delighted that he had noticed. She knew she had his curiosity aroused and loved seeing such an impatient pout on his face.

"She doesn't think little boys should hear," Joey pointed out, unperturbed. "You know there are certain things kids aren't supposed to know."

This insightful remark of Joey's intrigued Leslie, and she was just about to ask him if he had any idea as to why that was, when a young man casually strode over to where they were sitting and asked if he could join them.

"Sure, Kevin, pull up a chair," Randy said, indicating the grass beside him. "Goodness, I haven't seen you in quite a while. Leslie, this is my cousin, Kevin Smith, Aunt Amy and Uncle Anthony's boy. Or should I say man—after all, you are nearing thirty now, aren't you?"

"Nearly over the hill, soon to join you on the other side," Kevin replied, then glanced again at Leslie and added, "My, but you found yourself a good-looking woman. I gather she's your fiancée?"

"No, we aren't engaged," said Randy.

"Yet," Leslie added, opening her eyes wide when she realized she had said that thought out loud. Glancing surreptitiously toward Randy to find out what his reaction was, she couldn't tell which he was straining more, his wide-open eyes or his gaping mouth. Hiding a smile, she took another bite of her hamburger.

"Oh, when's the big event?"

"Yes, when?" Randy wanted to know.

Kevin gave Randy an inquiring look as if wondering

why Leslie seemed to know all about this and he did not. They both waited for her to finish her mouthful of hamburger to hear her answer.

"You two really getting married?" Joey asked, attention temporarily distracted from his corn. Randy looked at Leslie and waited for her to answer that question, too.

"We've discussed it" was all she would say on the matter and promptly changed the subject, leaving Randy feeling terribly frustrated and more than curious. She was getting such devious pleasure from his perplexed expression. "Tell me, Kevin, were you and Randy very close when you were boys?"

While Randy and Kevin first reminisced and then brought each other up to date on their lives, Leslie watched Randy from the new perspective she had. She was hardly able to restrain herself from declaring her love and newfound desire to be his wife and have his children. It was obvious he sensed some change in her by the way his eyes kept returning to stare curiously at her. No longer interested in her food by the time Joey got up to scrounge seconds, she asked him to dispose of her plate for her.

The only thing that worried Leslie at this point was how suddenly her attitude had changed. Could anything that occurred that quickly be real? She wished she had someone to discuss it with, and she was never so delighted to see Carol than when she came trotting up moments later. Although she knew she would not be able to talk to her at the moment, it was a comforting feeling to know her friend was close by.

"Sorry we're late," Carol said breathlessly as she made herself comfortable on the grass beside them.

"Aren't you going to get something to eat?" Randy asked looking around to see where Tommy was.

"Tommy's supposed to be seeing if you vultures left anything worth eating."

Within minutes, Tommy had joined them, awkwardly carrying two heaping plates and two drinks. He carefully handed down one of each, then eased down beside Carol.

While they ate, Tommy and Carol kept exchanging knowing smiles. Randy watched the silent exchange between the two and finally had to ask, "What is it with everybody today? Has spring fever hit months early? Everyone's acting so wacky."

"Wacky, huh?" Tommy mused, then, looking to Carol, he asked, "Do you want to tell them or do you want me to?" It was easy to see that Tommy wanted to be the one to announce their news.

Having received a go-ahead nod from Carol, Tommy said, beaming, "Carol and I are thinking about getting married this summer. We talked about it on the way over, and we both seem to like the idea. What do you think?"

"I think you must have some magical power to have been able to win her over this fast," Randy commented. Then, in a deep authoritative voice, he asked, "But do you love her, boy?"

"Yes, sir," Tommy replied with a serious nod.

Then Randy turned to Carol and asked, "Can you cook Mexican food and do you promise to invite me over regularly?"

Carol laughed. "Yes, sir."

"Then you have my blessing."

Tommy sighed with exaggerated relief, then chuckled. "Then we really can get married. Thank you." He placed his hand over his heart in a melodramatic gesture. "But we're still just talking about it. We haven't made any definite plans yet."

"Well, when you do make it definite, remember your older brother when trying to think of a best man."

Leslie was stunned and a little worried that Carol might not have thought this thing through. Carol was too much of a free spirit to be thinking so seriously about tying herself down to one man. Or was that just part of the old phobia cropping up again? Leslie wondered if she was really so sure *she* should be thinking about marriage. Shouldn't she worry about how suddenly her attitude had changed? What she and Carol needed to do was get together and talk about this, and the sooner the better. Before either of them made any definite plans that included marriage, they needed to be certain it was what they wanted. Marriage should not be entered into lightly.

"Well, Leslie, don't you have anything to say?" Carol wanted to know, breaking her concentration.

"Does this mean you'll be moving to Marshall?"

"Yes. If we get married, his business far outranks my job, and we would want to live in Marshall. But don't look so worried. We would still be seeing a lot of each other. Especially if you and Randy ever finally decide to get married. Then we would see each other at every family gathering. And the Brinnads are big on family gatherings."

"It may be sooner than you think," Randy piped in. "You aren't the only two who have been talking about marriage today."

"Hey, great—maybe we can make it a double wedding." Tommy said happily.

"I don't know. It might be too confusing. I'd hate to find out when it was all over that I had accidentally gotten myself married to two women. Besides, Leslie has only hinted at it—we haven't actually made any real commitments. But I'm eager as can be to get to that." He gave Leslie a quick loving look.

"Ah, you're just eager to get your hands on all her money," Tommy kidded.

"It's not her money I wanted to get my hands on,' Randy said, with a wicked flutter of his brows. Everyone laughed at his remark.

"I know what you mean," Tommy agreed. "I've beem wanting to get my hands on something of Carol's, too—the rest of her hamburger. I'm starved."

"Just my luck," Carol mumbled in a flat tone.

When Joey returned moments later with his second plate full of food and a very attentive shaggy dog at his heels, the conversation took a drastic turn. The little boy seemed intent on discussing the possibility of finding snakes, frogs and lizards on such a warm day, making everyone feel a little uneasy about the grassy area they had chosen to sit in. Soon they were all up and socializing again.

Chapter Ten

Having gotten little sleep the night before was taking its toll on Leslie as she attempted to concentrate on the report in front of her. A dull ache had started in the right side of her head, and it seemed to be progressing despite the aspirins she had taken over an hour ago. While she tried to keep working, her thoughts kept straying to Randy and how her conversation had gone with Carol last night. Not only had she discovered that Carol had always hoped to find the right man and get married, but that she herself really liked the idea of getting married to Randy. But because the conversation had lasted so long and it had gotten to be very late before they were through, she had not been able to talk to Randy about any of it.

Leslie had wanted to have that heart-to-heart with Carol first, so she had declined Randy's invitation to go over to his house to visit for a little while after they had let Joey off. For the first time in weeks he had seemed eager to be alone with her, but she had wanted to be absolutely sure of her heart before making a commitment to him. If she had gone to his house, she might have felt pressed to decide one way or the other. She had actually lied to him and told him that she wanted to get home because she had a bad headache. Justly, that headache was now becoming a reality. Laying down her pencil, she began to massage her temples, then the tight muscles at the base of her neck. She could no longer stare down at the pages of dot matrix print. It only seemed to intensify the pain.

"Cassie, would you please bring me another pencil?" She realized she had just broken the point on the one she'd been using and her pencil holder was empty.

"Will do" came her secretary's cheerful reply.

Closing her eyes a moment, Leslie wished she had been able to get more sleep. Even though she could try to blame her inability to fall asleep last night on her noisy neighbors and the paper-thin walls, she knew the real reason had been because her mind simply would not turn off. Despite the fact that she had left Carol's thinking she knew what she wanted, she began worrying again that she might be making a mistake in marrying Randy, and then she worried that she would be making a mistake if she didn't. If there was something she could think of to worry about, she had worried about it last night. Should she or shouldn't she? It was a mental tug-of-war that had lasted all night and left Leslie feeling drained and her nerves on edge.

"Here're a couple of pencils all sharpened and ready to go," Cassie said, laying them in front of Leslie. "How's the headache?"

"Worse," Leslie admitted.

"Why don't you go on home and rest?"

"No, I have two appointments scheduled for this morning."

"Nothing I can't cancel."

"No, I know how I hate to have something canceled on me at the last minute."

Cassie shook her head and went quietly back to her desk. She knew how to read her boss and realized that Leslie was not going to be talked into leaving her office when she felt she had a personal responsibility to be there.

An hour or so passed, and Leslie managed to get through the first meeting just fine. She had found it hard to concentrate fully on what the sales representative had to say, but she had done her best.

Now she sat with her head down on her desk blotter frantically rubbing her forehead. The pain was pervasive but seemed to center in her forehead and along the upper region of her skull. The throbbing had grown so severe that tears were forming in her eyes even when she squeezed her lids shut. She could not remember ever having had a headache quite this severe. The pain was so strong that she couldn't think of anything else, not even Randy.

"Leslie, what's wrong?" Her mother's voice cut through the fog of pain that surrounded her.

"I have a headache."

"You look terrible. You're pale as a ghost. I want you to go home right now and lie down. What you need is rest and a little peace and quiet."

"That's something I won't get at my place," she croaked out, hoping to sound lighthearted but realizing her feeble voice had revealed the true agony she was in. "I'm apt to get more peace and quiet right here."

"Then go lie down in your old room at my house. You'll get plenty of peace and quiet there. Randy can see to it."

"But I have an appointment with Mr. Trent soon," she explained, lifting her head, only to find that the stabbing pain was working its way down the back of her neck as well.

"I can take care of Mr. Trent," her mother assured her. "You don't buy that much from him anyway. I'll stay right here in your office and take care of anything and everything that crops up. I'm perfectly capable. I don't have anything important planned for today anyway. Get out of here."

Leslie no longer wanted to argue. For once she would gladly do as she was told. She did not even realize how her mother had actually taken charge for a change. All she could concentrate on was the pain. "I appreciate this, Mom. I really would like to lie down for a while."

"Then get out of here," her mother repeated, handing Leslie her jacket and purse. "Do you need me to drive you home? Or Cassie could take you."

"No, I can make it," she assured her mother, gratefully accepting her things, then left.

By the time Leslie reached her mother's house, her head felt as if it were going to explode. Weak from the severity of the pain, she made her way to the front door, not bothering to park in the garage. She wanted to get to bed as quickly as possible, and the front door provided the shortest route.

"Randy, bring some aspirin to my room," she called out as she stumbled toward the stairway. It had not been four hours since she had taken the last ones, but she did not really care. The first ones had not worked anyway.

"Randy?"

There was no answer. Damn. Where was he? Couldn't he hear her?

"Randy!" she called out again, wincing with the resulting pain.

"Randy, where are you?" Again her head exploded from the extra exertion it had taken to shout.

"Randy, where the hell are you?"

The pain was intolerable. Placing both hands on her head as if attempting to hold it together, she proceeded to the kitchen. It was after eleven—he should be in the kitchen preparing lunch by now. Why hadn't he heard her?

"Randy?" Her voice sounded far away to her. It was as if she were walking through a tunnel. She looked around the room, but there was no sign of him, and nothing was out of place. Unable to remember if his car had been outside when she drove up, she went to the door and peered through the window. There sat the red coupe in its usual place, but she noticed that the garage door was up and her mother's station wagon was gone. Where had he gone, and why? She knew that today was not errand day—tomorrow and Thursdays were errand days unless something unusual came up. He was supposed to be here, working. Her mother had said he would be here to help her.

Angry that he was not there when she needed help,

and angry that he had the gall to take her mother's station wagon without permission, Leslie let out a high-
pitched scream that sent another spasm wrenching
through her head.

Randy was gone. Apparently he was not at all the
dedicated employee he had pretended to be. He was
skipping out in the mornings to do heaven knew what
while they were away at work. What other things had
he pretended? Hot tears streamed down her cheeks
while she made her way up the stairs to find the aspirin
herself.

Locating a bottle of aspirin in her mother's bathroom, Leslie swallowed two of them and went only as
far as her mother's bed to lie down. Despite the pain
and anger she was suffering, sleep quickly overcame
her, and it was hours before a loud noise woke her.
When she blinked awake, she realized she had heard a
door close not far away, and now she heard footsteps
coming down the hallway.

"There you are," Randy said when he leaned through
the doorway and saw her lying on the bed. When he
stepped inside, Leslie noticed he still had her mother's
keys in his hands, and that reminded her that he had
been gone when she arrived.

"I wondered where you were," he said. "I saw your
car out front, but then I couldn't find you. Are you
feeling ill? What's wrong? Why isn't your mother
here?"

Leslie ignored his questions. She had several of her
own.

"Randy, where have you been?" she asked, her
words clipped and her voice biting. She gave the keys in

his hand a pointed glance. "No wonder you like this job so much. Being totally unsupervised in the mornings gives you great leeway to do exactly what you want. As long as you slip back in here in time to have something prepared for our lunch by one, you can get away with whatever you like. What other benefits have you helped yourself to?"

Randy stared at her, narrowing his eyes against her harsh words. He remained silent, gazing at her with an unfathomable expression. It was not anger exactly, and it certainly was not fear. What was it?

Sitting up, Leslie was aware that her headache was better. Although the area along the back of her neck still seemed very tender, the throbbing had stopped. Standing up, she confronted him face to face.

"Well, Randy, aren't you going to say something in your own defense?"

"Barky was hit by a car." His expression never changed, but suddenly Leslie recognized it for what it was. Sadness. He looked emotionally drained.

"Oh, no—is he dead?" She was aghast at the thought.

"No, he's alive, but one of his back legs was broken, his ribs are badly bruised, and one of them is shattered."

"What happened?"

"He chased a soccer ball out into the street and was run over. Hit-and-run. The jerk didn't even slow down to see if he could help. Joey came running in the kitchen screaming hysterically that Barky was hurt, and I ran out to see what had happened. The dog was alive, but he couldn't get up. He yelped out in pain every time he tried. Since I couldn't fit the dog and Joey into my car comfortably, I borrowed Margaret's station wagon. I knew she wouldn't mind, considering the circumstances. I wanted Barky to be able to lie flat.''

"But where was Joey's grandmother during all this?"

"Down the block, visiting a friend. I didn't want to waste time trying to find her. I needed to get Barky to a vet as quickly as possible almost as much for Joey's sake as the dog's. Joey was going to pieces watching his dog suffer. I took them to that animal hospital halfway between here and my house. We stayed until they were able to tell us how extensive his injuries were. I was so afraid that little dog was going to die or have to be put to sleep.''

Tears had started to form in Randy's eyes. As he tried to continue, his voice began to waver and his face tightened. ''It broke my heart to watch Joey's anguish while we waited. He kept remembering the time he had waited with his mother in a room much like the one we were in the night his father had died. If they had come out and announced that the dog was going to die, I don't know what I would have done to comfort Joey. Barky means the world to that boy.''

"Randy, I'm so sorry," Leslie strained to say. Tears had formed in her eyes as well, and an undeniable tightness gripped her throat. She could barely swallow.

Then, stepping forward to comfort him, she asked, "And—Barky's condition?"

Randy wrapped his arms around her and hugged her to him. Holding him close, she could feel him trembling in her arms. He was suffering from the aftereffects of having held in so much intense emotion for so long.

"He'll have to spend a few days at the animal hospital before they'll let him come home, but he's going to be fine. Good as new, the vet said."

"I feel like such a heel, accusing you the way I did. I don't know what came over me. I've been pretty emotionally wound up these days. I'm so sorry."

He loosened his grip in order to look at her. She could see that his tears had built up until they were on the verge of spilling over, and was aware that her own tears had already blazed wet trails down her cheeks. He buried his face in her hair as if suddenly trying to hide his vulnerability.

"Where is Joey now?" she asked softly.

Although his words were muffled by her hair, she was able to understand him. "His grandmother was home by the time we got back. I left him with her."

For a long time Leslie simply held him. She waited until he was ready to pull away. When he did, he quickly turned away from her and apologized for having lost control the way he had, claiming it was ridiculous.

"I understand," she assured him, placing her hands lightly on his shoulders. Although he was not facing her, she could meet his eyes in the mirror over her mother's dresser. "Look at me. I'm not exactly the pillar of strength here. I cried just hearing about it." She smiled, wiping the tears from her face with the back of her hand. In all honesty, she had liked seeing the vulnerable side of Randy. She had never felt closer to him than she did at that moment. Leaning against his back, she pressed her damp cheek into the soft material of his flannel shirt. "I know how fond you are of Joey. I'd think you were a rather heartless man if you hadn't

been affected. It just proves something I've always suspected but could never quite be sure of.''

''And what's that?''

''That you're human.''

She could hear his laughter through the ear pressed
against his back, and it made her smile. It was such a
deep and golden sound.

''So you've had your doubts about that, have you?''
Quickly, he turned to face her. Although his eyes were
still slightly reddened, they sparkled with mirth. ''If it
weren't for your stupid rules, I'd show you just how
human I am.''

Looking away first, she finally found the courage to
return her gaze to the crystal blue of Randy's eyes. Leslie smiled up at him. She felt suddenly shy but bold
enough to speak.

''I've always heard it said that most rules are meant
to be broken.''

Randy let out his usual low growl and clasped her in
his arms again. His lips descended on hers with such a
wild and urgent passion that Leslie moaned aloud with
the pleasure it brought her. She burned with sweet ecstasy, and eagerly she wrapped her arms around him
and hugged him close. Feeling impelled to let him
know she was hungry for more, she pressed her lips
harder against his. She had starved for his kisses long
enough. Eagerly she hoped he would make a move toward the bed. She so wanted to share the ultimate expression of love with him. She had dreamed about it
long enough—the time had come to know the bound-
less rapture of their love.

Pulling his lips free of hers, he breathed heavily

against her cheek. His hands still held her firmly against him. Leslie looked up to see that his eyes were squeezed tight. The muscles in his jaw were rigid, working furiously as though he was angry or hurt.

"What's wrong?"

"I can't take advantage of you like this."

Not again! In all the movies she had ever seen and in all the romances she had ever read, it was the woman who always found reason to pull away, never the man. It was the man who always whispered the sweet nothings in the woman's ears while the woman whispered sweet nothings in his.

"You won't be taking advantage of me, Randy. I want you."

"After what just happened, I can't be certain that you want me for the right reasons and are not simply wanting to console me, to comfort me at a time when I showed weakness. If any part of your willingness to make love stems from a need to comfort me or give me strength, it wouldn't be right. It's too important to me that it be love—true and undeniable love—that finally brings us together."

"Maybe it is love," she offered, clinging to him.

"And again maybe it isn't love, but a strange sort of sympathy you feel. I can't take that chance." Pressing his lips firmly against her forehead, he held her a minute before pulling away. Still clutching the keys, he went over to the dresser and returned them to where they were always kept.

"How about a little lunch? I know it's late, but I can prepare something simple in a matter of minutes," he offered. His voice had an unnatural quality to it.

Leslie glanced around at the digital clock on the nightstand beside her mother's bed. It was already past two. Now that her headache was nearly gone, she felt she should be getting back to work. But something kept her from mentioning that to Randy.

"I am a little hungry. Lunch would be nice if you would agree to eat with me and keep me company. I don't care to eat alone, and Mother won't be here. She's busy at Lovall's."

"I guess it wouldn't hurt for me to eat with you this once." Randy usually refused to join her or her mother in meals at the house because he did not feel the hired help should take meals with employers. Away from the house was different—he was no longer an employee.

It was after three when they finally finished eating their soup and sandwiches, and Leslie realized that she was still in no hurry to get back to work. It worried her that she could feel so apathetic toward her duties. Lovall's had always held top priority with her, as it should—why now was she so reluctant to return? She knew it had to do with Randy, and that troubled her. Finally her conscience won out, and she went upstairs to run a brush through her hair and get the jacket she had flung carelessly across a chair in her mother's room.

"I promised to take Joey by the animal hospital as soon as I get off. He wants to make sure Barky's still all right. It closes at six. Then I told him we could go to Burger King for supper. Would you care to join us?" Randy asked, having followed her upstairs.

"No, I doubt I'll be finished working in time. I'll have quite a bit of catching up to do." Actually, she still had quite a bit of thinking to do, and the next time she was with Randy, she wanted them to be alone, because they would have a lot of talking to do.

By four o'clock she was back at her desk, still unable to concentrate on the work piled on her desk. Her mind continued to be plagued with unending thoughts of Randy. She couldn't help but play with the thought of what would have happened if he hadn't made her stop. Would they have made love? What would it have been like? She couldn't seem to stop daydreaming about it.

That night Leslie managed to get to sleep with little effort, and next morning there was absolutely no trace of her headache. She felt terrific. When she got to her mother's, just before eight, Leslie was amused and slightly embarrassed to find Randy wearing a brand-new dark-blue T-shirt that said in bold white letters "Rules are meant to be broken." When he entered the dining room with their breakfast in hand, he smiled at her and gave the message on his shirt a quick glance to make sure she had noticed it.

"You look as if you're feeling a lot better this morning," he sang out, scooping the steaming plates off the tray and placing one in front of her and the other in front of Margaret.

"The headache's gone, but I still have this nagging pain in my neck." She couldn't help grinning.

"You aren't referring to me, are you?"

"How perceptive you are!" She laughed, aware that her mother was paying special attention to this strange conversation.

"How do you like my new shirt?" he asked as he poured orange juice first in Margaret's glass then in hers, letting his arm brush against hers and raising goose bumps on her skin. He was clearly letting her know that her don't-touch rule was out, and she was delighted.

"It's very—blue," she replied, stifling a chuckle.

Margaret waited until Randy had returned to the kitchen before boldly asking what all *that* was about.

"Nothing much."

Margaret eyed her daughter a long moment before speaking again. Then she said, "Where does it stand between you and Randy? You two have been seeing quite a lot of each other for well over two months now. Is there any chance it's getting serious?"

Leslie just looked at her. She did not know what to say. There were some things you simply did not discuss with your mother. She would feel awkward, to say the least, if she were to admit that she cared deeply for Randy and even had fantasies in which they made mad, passionate love to each other. What would her mother think if she knew that her very own daughter would have been more than willing to make love to her handsome housekeeper right in her mother's very own bed? No, there were certain things a mother was better off not knowing.

When Leslie didn't bother to answer her, Margaret prompted her further. "I'm not blind to the fact that you two are constantly exchanging flirtatious little glances and have odd things to say to each other. After all, I'm not dead, you know. Doyle has proved that to me."

"Oh, he has, has he? And just how has he done that?" she asked, hoping to change the subject. If there was anything that Margaret liked to talk about, it was Doyle.

"He's shown me how much life still has to offer," Margaret said, smiling, a distant look in her eyes. "He's brought laughter back into my life, and that's something that's been missing since your father died. Doyle has not only shown me that I still have a little life left in me, but he's also changed the way I view that life. And in these last few months I've seen great changes in your attitude, which I think are directly attributed to that handsome young man in there. You seem happier and are certainly much easier to get along with. I felt that he was the perfect man for you almost immediately."

She paused, carefully scrutinizing her daughter. "Did something I should know about happen yesterday while you two were here alone?"

"Mother!" Why was she feeling so embarrassed by this?

Margaret shrugged. "I like Randy. I think he would make a wonderful son-in-law. I just want to know how you feel about him."

'I like Randy, too. And you could be right, he might make a wonderful son-in-law," she conceded, not aware that he had reentered the room just in time to hear her every word.

"Is that a proposal?" he asked casually, coming forward with a small carafe of steaming coffee for Margaret. "If so, I would like a little time to think it over. Marriage is a big step, you know. I don't know if I'm ready to get tied down like that and give up my independence."

Leslie sighed heavily, then turned to give him another one of her pointed looks. "You know rules and teeth have a lot in common, Randy, dear. While some people like to go around breaking someone else's rules, other people find gratification in smashing up something more substantial, like teeth, or even noses, or perhaps jawbones." She smiled sweetly as she gave the message time to soak in.

"Gotcha." He grinned, deepening his dimples, and quickly poured Margaret's coffee before retreating again to the safety of the kitchen.

To Leslie's delight, things were getting back to the way they had been before Randy's decision to follow her stupid rules. He was again teasing her and taunting her and—best of all—touching her whenever they were alone, ignoring her dire warnings and threats. As the days passed, she became aware that not only was he touching her again, she was suddenly finding nearly as many reasons to touch him, too. She liked having bodily contact with him, even if it was only a simple touch, a brief brushing of arms or bumping of shoulders. It would send electrical currents shooting through her, causing her blood to race.

That next Saturday afternoon, Leslie was not at all surprised to find Randy at her door. She had barely been home from work fifteen minutes and there he was, wanting her to go with him to the mall. His eyes glittered with excitement as he explained the purpose of the trip. He wanted to get Joey a little red wagon.

"And why does Joey need a wagon?"

"We went over to the animal hospital this afternoon to get Barky. The vet told us to keep him quiet and not to let him run around for a week or so. Even though he's heavily bandaged, they want him to remain still.''

"So why the wagon? I don't get it.''

"You know how Barky wants always to be near Joey. You hardly ever see one without the other. Barky will be trying to get up and walk in order to stay at Joey's side. He isn't about to be left behind. I figure if Joey makes Barky a bed in the wagon, he can move him from room to room and even outside without the dog doing damage to his wounds. Anyway, it's worth a try.''

Leslie did not even take time to change her clothes. Catching fire from Randy's enthusiasm, she went with him to the mall and helped him choose a little red wagon with wooden rails all the way around the top. They had gone in her car, knowing full well they were never going to get a wagon to fit into his. They stopped by Randy's house to get an old pillow he remembered was in his hall closet, then they headed for Joey's grandmother's, where Joey and Barky were supposed to be spending the weekend. As usual, his mother was going to be out of town on a business trip.

When they rang the doorbell, Joey's grandmother, Jane Langford, was the one who greeted them. Joey was not leaving Barky's side even to answer the door for fear the dog would try to follow and tear the stitches where he had had to have surgery to remove a fragment of his rib from his lung. When they entered the living room, they found the two lying on the floor nose to nose. One of Barky's hind legs was bandaged, and there was a large bandage around his middle. A lot of his shaggy hair had been shaved near the bandages.

Turning only his eyes, still half hidden by hair, to see who had entered, Barky looked pitiful.

"How's it going?" Randy asked cheerfully as he entered, carrying the wagon.

"He hurts. When he tried to get up a while ago, he yelped loud," Joey said sadly, not bothering to look up. "I can't even get up without him wanting to try to follow me. Poor guy."

"You knew that was going to be a problem. That's why we got this."

"A wagon?" Joey said curiously when he finally looked up. Then as if he could read Randy's mind, he exclaimed, "A wagon!"

"Think he'll go for it?"

"I'll ask him," Joey said, turning his face back to the dog's. "How about it, Barky? Do you want your own set of wheels? Now you can go wherever I go."

Barky lifted his head and looked toward Randy as he put the wagon on the floor nearby. Looking back at Joey, the dog's tail began to pat against the floor enthusiastically. Leslie, finding herself a little amazed, wondered how much the dog actually understood.

"We've put a nice soft pillow in there for you to lie on," Randy explained as he got down on all fours between the dog and the wagon.

Carefully, while Joey's grandmother watched, Randy, Leslie and Joey lifted Barky, keeping him as level as they could. The dog was quiet until they laid him comfortably on the pillow, then he barked out his appreciation.

"How's that?" Randy wanted to know. Still on all fours, he had lowered his chin so that he was eye-level with Barky.

"He likes it," Joey told him.

"Well, let's try it out," Randy said eagerly, and lifted the handle so Joey would take it. With Randy walking beside them on his knees, Joey pulled a delighted Barky around the living room. The dog barked out his excitement, and each time Randy came back with an appropriate comment, making Joey laugh again and again. When they returned to the spot where they had started, Joey turned to Randy and threw his little arms around him, hugging him tight.

"Thank you, Mr. Randy. Thank you so much."

Leslie knew Randy had closed his eyes to fight back the tears as he gave his strained reply, "You're welcome, Joey, you're welcome so much."

They stayed over an hour, making sure Barky was comfortable in his new bed on wheels. Leslie joined in on occasion whenever Joey insisted she give Barky a pull around the room, but mainly she stood back with Joey's grandmother and watched. It was heartwarming to watch Randy and Joey. She could not help realizing what a wonderful father Randy would make. He was so caring.

That night, after they had left Joey, Leslie seemed to settle into a sort of euphoria, having been with Randy and Joey and having watched them smile and laugh together. Randy was special. And having seen the way he was with Joey, she not only felt he would make a wonderful father, she knew he would make a wonderful husband as well. She could not help envisioning what it would be like being married to Randy, with a family of their own.

As she drove Randy back over to her apartment,

where he had left his car, he noticed the faraway look and the half smile on her face. He had spoken once to her and she hadn't even heard him.

"Earth to Leslie. Earth to Leslie," he chanted into an imaginary microphone. "Come in, Leslie."

Realizing he had caught her daydreaming, she let her half smile grow into a full smile and admitted, "I was lost in thought. Sorry."

"What were you thinking of?" he wanted to know, joining her in her smile even though he had no idea why.

"Do you really want to know?"

"I wouldn't have asked."

"I was wondering what it would be like to be married to you and have a family of our own, possibly a little boy like Joey. I was thinking what a great father you would make."

Randy's eyes opened wide with amazement. He clearly had not expected that answer. "You were?"

"Yes, in my mind I was pretending we were married, with kids of our own."

"And what was it like?"

"Kinda nice, actually." Her smile broadened even further.

"Nice enough to really consider?"

Pulling into a vacant parking spot near her apartment, she paused until she had stopped the car. "Yes, nice enough to really consider."

Randy swallowed and started to speak, but words did not come out, only a strangled noise. When he realized that words were failing him miserably, he finally fell silent. Looking at her with astonishment, he allowed his eyes to search hers as if looking for something specific, something he could build hope on.

"Want to come in and talk about it?"

Randy still had not found enough voice to form words, but he nodded vigorously. Reaching immediately for the door handle, he was out of the car and at her front door in an instant. Indeed, he did want to come in and discuss it. He was eager to hear more.

Chapter Eleven

"It's been so long since we've been alone without having someone right in the next room or in the backseat that it feels almost strange," Leslie commented as she flipped on the overhead lights and waited for Randy to come in. "We haven't had a real chance to talk."

"There was a reason for that," he told her, grinning sheepishly.

"There was? What?"

"I was afraid I wouldn't be able to stick to my promise to keep my hands off you if we were ever totally alone again. Having someone else around removed certain temptations for me. The truth is, I was afraid to be alone with you. I'm not the greatest when it comes to willpower." His blue eyes shimmered with candor as he explained.

Leslie stared at him while she gently closed the door. So that was why he was always so eager to invite Tommy and Carol or little Joey to join them. Thank heavens.

"I thought you were just getting bored with me. So much so, you wanted someone else along to help liven things up. I must admit, I was afraid you were simply losing interest in being alone with me anymore.''

''Oh, I was interested all right. Too interested. And I was afraid a moment alone with you would prove to be my doom. I had stated I could go without touching you, and I was determined to keep my word.''

''Hmm. Well, we're alone now and the rule no longer applies. What do you think we should do about that?'' she taunted him, wetting her lips with the tip of her pink tongue in a most provocative manner.

''Heaven help me, but I want to talk.'' Randy sighed heavily. ''I want to probe further into what we were discussing in the car out there.''

''And what was that? I can't seem to remember.''

''Let me remind you,'' he offered, then took her right arm in his and started humming the wedding march as he pretended to walk down an imaginary aisle that led them to the couch.

''Oh, marriage. I must have been talking about Tommy and Carol,'' she mused thoughtfully, placing a finger to her temple as if that might help her think. ''I was probably wondering what their wedding was going to be like. Or was I talking about Mother? The way she's been acting lately about her friend Doyle, she just might be thinking about getting married soon.''

''No, that's not exactly what you indicated was on your mind,'' he commented, warning her with his purposeful expression. ''Seems to me you said something about considering what it would be like to be married to yours truly. You even went so far as to mention children.''

"Oh, that. You don't really want to hear about that, do you?"

Pulling her down on the couch, he sat leaning over her and lowered his eyebrows in a menacing manner. "I have ways of making you talk."

"That's a lousy German accent, but it does sound intriguing."

Shaking his head, he moaned, "You're driving me nuts."

Leslie considered that, then leaned up and placed a brief kiss on his cheek then smiled. "Okay, I'll talk. It's just that I don't know exactly how or where to begin."

"Begin with the part about your being willing to consider marriage to me. Were you serious or were you priming me for some sort of cruel joke?"

"I honestly think I was serious." She nodded in amazement. It certainly was a turnaround for her. "I've become fairly accustomed to the idea of marriage."

"You *think* you were serious?" he asked, sounding suddenly doubtful. He looked crestfallen, and his shoulders sagged a little. She was still not certain.

"I *know* I was serious," she amended with a reassuring smile. "Still am. Lately, I've thought a lot about you and me in terms of our having a real future together. I've concluded that I'm hopelessly in love with you, Randy Brinnad, and have been for some time now, but I was afraid to admit it even to myself. In fact, Carol realized it was love I was feeling for you even before I did."

"But is it love?"

"It has to be. What else can it be? I can think of nothing else. You're on my mind constantly. So much so I can hardly sleep nights."

"You sure indigestion isn't your problem? That sort of sticks with you and can really mess up your sleep."

"Yes, I'm sure. There's a simple cure for indigestion and there is no simple cure for what I feel for you."

"And you are really willing to consider marrying me?" He was in awe. When had she changed her mind?

"Very willing."

"What about your fear of becoming overly dependent on someone?"

"I'm afraid I'm already at that point or I've passed it. Despite my desire to keep my life in balance—on a steady, even course, so to speak—some sorry devil named Randy Brinnad entered my life and started rocking my safe and serene little boat until I finally capsized. Now I find myself floundering constantly in a deep, turbulent sea of emotions. I tried my best to fight the rising tide, but I've found myself going down for the third time. I struggled to keep my life just the way it was—comfortable, predictable, and mostly uneventful, afraid of change. Yet it was a hopeless battle. You don't exactly play fair."

"Hey, I gave fair play a shot. I found it highly unenjoyable, but I did try it there for a while."

"Yes, I know, and you became so darned honorable that I nearly went insane. I hated it—you were always near but never touching. Pure torture."

"What about me? I've never had to take so many cold showers in my life. Granted, I saved a fortune on my hot-water bill but ran my electric bill way up burning the lights until the wee hours all those nights I couldn't sleep."

"So did I. Just think how much money we could save on utilities if we were to get married."

"Is that a proposal? What about your belief that committing yourself to one person and coming to depend on that one person is not for you? What about your dedication to never being confined in such a way?"

Looking thoughtful for a moment, Leslie answered, "I no longer see our relationship as confining. Actually, it can be better termed as expanding. I've grown in so many ways since I met you. I used to view that sort of total commitment as a weakness, especially in women, but I've come to see it very differently."

"How so?"

"I honestly view it as an added strength. I've always considered myself a rather strong person, but now I have your strength to draw from as well. Together I see us as invincible."

"What about your fear of losing your identity and your freedom?"

"I realize now that I won't be losing my identity at all. I might find myself changing it a bit now and then, but I doubt I'll ever lose me. I don't think you're the type to demand I knuckle under to outlandish demands. I've come to trust you. I'm no longer afraid of what my life will be like if I share it with you. In fact, I'm eager to find out. And as for freedom, I want the freedom to be able to share my love with you anytime and anywhere. Marriage can give me that freedom."

"Hmm—a license to love?"

"Exactly."

"And are you willing to give me your all?"

"Every inch." She smiled sensually. "You can have my heart, my soul and whatever else interests you."

Randy's mouth formed the word "wow," but no sound came out. He bit his lower lip in an effort to control himself.

"Looks like we're about to check out this happy-ever-after business," Leslie said enthusiastically. "I can see us now, living in a huge house with a superlarge garage so you can have plenty of room to tinker with your old cars."

"What's wrong with my house? I thought you really liked my place. It's plenty large. Maybe later on, if we have so many kids my house won't hold them all, we might look for a larger place, but I kinda like the idea of the two of us living in my house. And that garage meets my needs well enough. Besides, if our house was too large, I might have to spend too much time looking for you."

Slipping her arms around his shoulders, she said in a silky voice, "You won't have any trouble finding me, no matter what size our home is. Your problem will most likely be getting rid of me long enough to find a moment's peace. And, yes, I do love your house and can't wait to make it our home." She just wanted him to have the best. He certainly deserved it.

Randy leaned forward and placed tiny kisses on her forehead and cheeks that made her tingle right down to her toes. Then he lifted his head back and looked at her for a long moment. "I can hardly believe this is happening. I was afraid it would take a lot longer than this to win you over."

Still tilting his head, he continued to gaze at her. Leslie grew worried when she noticed a tiny line tighten in Randy's forehead. She knew him well enough to know that he was concerned about something important.

"What's wrong?"

"You aren't letting what happened tonight with Joey and Barky influence you too much, are you? Your sudden decision to marry me isn't a direct result of all that joy bubbling up and spilling over, is it?"

"Maybe a little. But I've had fleeting thoughts of what it would be like to be married to you for several weeks."

"Fleeting?" He frowned. "Look, I don't want you to rush into anything. I want you to be absolutely certain you want to marry me. I want to give you plenty of time to consider all the pros and cons and know positively without a doubt that you love me. I want you to search deep into your very soul to be sure you want to spend the rest of your life with me. I'll give you three days. That should be plenty of time, don't you think?"

"Three whole days? How generous," she mused, nodding thoughtfully, not really sure what difference those three days could make anyway. She had no more doubts.

"Yes, in three days I will officially ask you for your hand in marriage. You have until then to decide what your answer will be."

"Then I have until Tuesday night to change my mind?"

"I don't like the way you worded that, but yes, you have until Tuesday night."

"Does that mean we have a date for Tuesday night?"

"How perceptive you are. Yes, we have a date, and we can go anywhere your heart desires. It should be someplace very special."

"Special, huh?"

"Where do you want to go?"

"Nowhere. I'd much rather prepare supper for you here."

It was decided. Tuesday evening at seven o'clock, Randy was to come over for supper and Leslie would have a definite decision for him, even though she already knew what that decision would be. She clearly wanted Randy, now and forever. But if it would make him feel more secure about this sudden change of heart for her to give it a few more days' thought, she would gladly oblige.

Sunday passed by in a blur. As soon as she dared, for Carol was a late sleeper, Leslie called her friend to tell her what had happened the night before. Carol became ecstatic and rushed to Leslie's apartment to talk with her in person. Eagerly they made all sorts of tentative plans for both their weddings and their futures, reverting back to schoolgirlhood now and again by bursting out in excited giggles. Later, when Tommy came over, then Randy, they all decided to go out to eat someplace special. After a bit of discussion, they decided to drive across the river into Bossier City to eat in the Atrium of the Le Bossier Hotel.

Leslie was particularly fond of the Atrium's exquisite food, as well as the live garden setting and natural lighting that gave the effect of being outdoors at the height of springtime. The faint rustling sound of trees and the musical sound of the cascading indoor waterfall added to the effect. It was such a serene setting, especially when contrasted to the vibrant excitement the four of them were experiencing.

Although the engagement was not truly official, Randy was eager to talk about his and Leslie's possible future. He was already thinking of names for their first-born. Leslie was quick to rule out Bernard and Bernadette as possibilities, for she couldn't stand the way they clashed with Brinnad. In the end, she made him promise to let her be the one to name their children should the occasion arise.

By Monday, Leslie was so aglow with the certainty of marriage that Cassie noticed it immediately.

"What happened to you this weekend? You sorta look like Garfield the cat after he's searched out and eaten an entire pan of lasagna."

It pleased Leslie to know that her happiness showed, and she gladly shared her news with her secretary. It was all she had been able to think about, and the more she talked about it the more real it seemed.

"I think I proposed marriage Saturday night," she said, and then she laughed, realizing it now seemed that way.

"You proposed marriage? And did he accept?"

"Sort of. He wants me to wait until Tuesday to be sure I wasn't talking out of my head."

"And were you?"

"Possibly. Isn't that the way with love?"

"Yes, I suppose it is," Cassie replied thoughfully, a knowing smile playing at her lips. "Who's the lucky guy?"

"His name is Randy Brinnad."

"Leslie Brinnad," Cassie said, experimenting with the sound of it. "We'll have to change the sign on both doors and get you a new desk plate."

Tapping the door plaque lightly, Leslie agreed. "Yes, we will, won't we?" Smiling at the thought, she retreated to the confines of her office.

Later, while Leslie was seated at her desk shuffling through the many tax forms that were due to be filled out soon, and looking over the previous year's records, which were supposed to help her in filling out those forms, she managed at last to get her mind off Randy and back on her work. It was a task not easily accomplished, but she was finally able to give the tax forms the full attention they demanded.

"You can't go in there unannounced, sir," she heard Cassie call out through the closed door.

Now what? She was having a hard-enough time trying to figure out all the year-end forms without having to deal with interruptions. Lifting her eyes to the door, she prayed that it did not open to admit an unwanted intruder. Moments later, the door did open, but the person barging in was not exactly unwanted. It was Randy.

"What are you doing here?" she asked, obviously surprised but welcoming him with a loving smile.

"Leslie, I tried to stop him, but he wouldn't listen," Cassie explained from somewhere behind Randy's left shoulder.

"That's all right, Cassie. This is Randy, the man I was telling you about earlier."

Randy's eyebrows raised with interest. "You've been discussing me, have you?" Then, turning to face

Cassie, he asked, "Just what is it she's been telling you about me? All sorts of terrible things, I'll bet. Do I possibly have grounds to sue? Do you think I'd be able to take her to court? Or maybe to bed?"

Cassie did not know how to take him and gave Leslie a worried glance.

"I never said he was normal," Leslie said with a chuckle, "but he's harmless. It's safe enough for you to go on back to your desk."

Cassie continued to give Randy a worried glance as she pulled the office door shut so they could have privacy. "Call if you need me."

"Why would I need her when I have you?" he asked, coming around Leslie's desk to stand beside her.

"She's talking to me," Leslie said, shaking her head. "Now, what are you doing here?"

Silent for a moment, Randy finally exploded. "Harmless? What kind of thing is that to say about a man?"

"Do you want an apology?" She laughed at her pouting fiancé. "Okay, I apologize. You're not harmless, but I stick by the fact that you're not normal. Now tell me why you're here."

"Your mother forgot her purse this morning and called to have me bring it to her."

"I'll bet you looked cute carrying in her purse!" Leslie laughed, conjuring up images of Randy with a large, pretentious purse on his arm or perhaps dangling from his hand.

"Hey, I might not be normal, but I'm not stupid. I was smart enough to put it in a paper bag," he boasted with a slight shake of his head. "When I passed by that hall door with your name on it as I was leaving, my curiosity got the best of me. I wanted to see where you work. I'm not disturbing you, am I?"

"You always disturb me," she admitted. Then, gesturing at the many papers scattered across her desk, she explained, "I was trying to decipher these tax forms. It's almost that time of year again."

"Trying?" he noted, glancing at the clutter on her desk. "What seems to be the problem?"

"The problem is that I haven't had to do this for a while. Last year I had an employee who knew how to do all this, but Nikki got married and moved to Dallas last November."

"I still don't see what the problem is. With Lovall's being on computer, your tax forms should be a breeze. Would you like me to help you?"

"That's right, you know accounting. Would you really be willing to help me with this?"

"What's in it for me?" he asked, letting his gaze drift downward to explore the curves her billowing blouse and tapered skirt concealed. His gaze lingered on her slender legs.

"The reward of having met a challenge head-on." She smiled sweetly, saluting the air with a determined fist. She had pretended not to have caught on to his poorly hidden meaning. Then, rising slowly from her chair, she reached for the top button of her blouse and boldly began to undo it. "Or if that isn't enough to make you want to help me with this, I can think of other rewards you might like."

Randy bit his lip in ill-concealed excitement when she undid the next three buttons and let her blouse gape open, revealing the wisp of French lace beneath.

"Deal!" he exclaimed eagerly, his eyes glued to the exposed softness. "In fact, you can consult me anytime. For rewards like that, I'll take over all of Lovall's bookwork."

"Are you serious? I thought you were through with desk work." For the first time, Leslie wondered what Randy's plans were as far as his job went. Did he plan to continue to be her mother's housekeeper? She supposed he did, but now she wondered if he might really be willing to help her manage Lovall's instead. She needed someone she could trust implicitly helping her manage the financial end of Lovall's, and Randy certainly was someone she felt she could trust. After all, she planned to marry him, didn't she?

"Hey, I'll do anything to take that frown off your pretty face and see that it doesn't return. Besides, look at the fringe benefits I'd get on this job."

"I'd appreciate it. I hate dealing with figures. Spreadsheets give me a headache and doing the monthly P and L makes me want to rip out my hair."

"And it would be a pity for you to rip out that lovely hair."

She smiled at his compliment, and continued. "Bookwork is the most antagonizing part of my job. It would mean a lot to me if you really would take over that part of Lovall's management entirely. It would not take up all your time, either. It won't be like when you worked at Walls'n'Rae. You wouldn't be stuck behind a desk except for a few hours a day. And you're right—you won't believe the fringe benefits." She raised a sultry eyebrow and reached for the next button on her blouse.

"You make it hard to say no," he rasped, moving

forward to drape his arms around her. "How do we break this bit of news to your mother? I hate leaving her high and dry."

"Can't you get your aunt to find a replacement? If not, I can always give Creel's another call. Mom will just have to understand that she is not simply losing a housekeeper, she's gaining a good accountant, and Lovall's can certainly use one."

"I'll see what I can do about getting your mother a replacement. I really like the idea of taking some of the work load off you to give you more free time for better things."

Later, during lunch, Randy mentioned he had things to do that evening and would probably not be seeing her. Not having received a reply from his aunt by lunchtime, they did not mention their plans to her mother then. He promised to call Leslie at work as soon as he knew anything for certain, and he did call her later that afternoon to confirm that his aunt would indeed have a replacement within a week.

"By the way, you haven't told your mother about the possibility that we just could be getting married, have you," he said, more as a statement of fact than a question.

"No, I haven't."

"Why?" he wanted to know, his voice sounding worried. Although she could not see his face, she knew that worry line was showing in his forehead. "You haven't started having second thoughts, have you?"

"Always the worrywart. I haven't told her because I want us to tell her together."

Randy let out a long breath, "Maybe we could go

over tomorrow night and tell her once it's official. That
is, if you haven't changed your mind. You haven't
changed it, have you?''

''You'll know tomorrow.''

''Leslie!''

''You're the one who wanted me to take three days,''
she reminded him.

''You are a cruel and heartless woman, Leslie Lovall,'' he muttered.

''And you love me.''

''Damn it.''

''See you tomorrow night at seven,'' she sang out,
then hung up. She had to admit, she was taking an evil
delight in making him suffer just a little.

When Tuesday night finally arrived, Leslie watched
Randy's bright red coupe pass through the parking lot
three times as he waited for seven o'clock to arrive. She
had had her Dijon steaks ready and simmering for
about ten minutes, and she alternately paced restlessly
and kept a vigil at the narrow slit in her curtain. It was
still ten minutes to seven, but the next time she saw his
car approaching, she rushed to the door to wave him in.

Quickly, he pulled into a vacant parking spot nearby
and got out of his car, carrying a huge bouquet of
flowers. Leslie could tell even from that distance that
the flowers were yellow daisies surrounded by tiny for-
get-me-nots. In his other hand was a tall narrow brown
sack. He hurried over to the door to greet her.

''Hi, gorgeous,'' he said before planting a warm kiss
on her forehead. ''I like that dress.''

Good. She had selected the long black dress because
of the seductive way it clung to her curves. It was one

of the most expensive gowns she owned, but she now felt it was well worth the price when she could see such open admiration on Randy's face. "Oh, this thing? It's just a little something I threw on," she said, batting her eyes, trying to do his famous innocent act justice.

"I hope it comes off as easily," he commented wryly. Then, presenting the flowers, he bowed slightly. "For you."

"How lovely." Leslie turned to put the flowers in a vase, leaving Randy to close the door. Next she put the champagne he had brought in the refrigerator to keep cold for later.

Since the meal was ready, they ate first, not so much as mentioning the main purpose of the evening. They both sensed that the time was not right. It was much later, after they had moved into the living room, that the subject finally arose. Having just lit the candles she had placed about the room, Leslie settled in next to Randy on the couch and snuggled close. His arm went automatically around her.

"This is nice," he commented, then pressed his lips into her hair. "Will you promise me if we get married that you will continue to prepare candlelight dinners every now and then?"

"What do you mean, *if*?" She smiled, leaning her head into his lips and enjoying the intimate pressure.

"Well, we haven't exactly settled that point, have we?"

"Isn't it about time we did?"

Gently pushing her away, he got up and walked over to the sack from which he had pulled the champagne bottle earlier, and which he had carefuly set aside.

He reached inside and retrieved a small box covered with dark-blue velvet. When he returned and knelt before her, he was unsuccessfully hiding a smile. In a dramatic gesture, he took her hand and kissed it.

"Will you, Leslie Lovall, woman of my dreams, marry me and bring pure joy and happiness to the rest of my life?"

Leslie couldn't help it. She laughed softly at the way Randy was overdoing it.

"You scoff at my affection?" A hand spread across his chest as if to protect his heart.

"Sorry," she said in a muffled voice, trying to control her laughter. When she finally did, she replied, "Why, sir, it would be an honor and a pleasure to marry you and bring joy and happiness to your life."

Presenting the box, he got up and rejoined her on the couch. He watched her as she carefuly examined the box and caressed its softness. Slowly, she opened it and gazed at the beauty of the golden wedding set. The rings were made of smooth gold, the engagement ring set with three smaller diamonds and the wedding band with one large diamond in the center and two smaller diamonds on either side. The rings were perfect.

"Randy, they're lovely," she said, admiring them, holding them so that the candlelight danced off the faceted surfaces of the stones.

"And you are absolutely sure that you want to marry me?"

She smiled lovingly at him. "I've never been more sure of anything in my life."

"This is too good to be true," he said, shaking his

head in doubt. "I love you so much. For a while I thought maybe too much."

"And I love you."

Taking the smaller ring from the box, he placed it on her finger. They both stared at it in awe for a moment before their eyes were once again drawn to each other.

"When do we get married?"

"How about April?" She smiled. "It will give our mothers enough time to make all the plans they want."

"That's over a month away," he complained. "I don't know if I can wait that long."

"To marry me?"

"To make love to you."

"Do you want to wait?"

"No."

"Then don't," she said in a smoky voice, setting the box that still held her wedding ring aside. Lifting her arms, she welcomed him. Their lips met in wondrous bliss. They both knew that this time neither of them would be turning back. This time when he pulled his lips free of her it was simply to express his love.

"Leslie, I never thought I could feel about anyone the way I feel about you. It's uncanny the way you've stirred my emotions. I love you so very much."

"And I love you just as much. It surprises even me, the depth of my love," she whispered before her lips sought his once more in a demanding kiss. Afraid to pull away from him lest the spell be broken, her next words seemed to come from the depths of her being. "You already have my heart and soul, you might as well have the rest of me."

His arms tightened around her, and Leslie responded by returning his powerful embrace. His tongue dipped into her mouth, teasing the inner edges of her lips, and she returned the favor in kind, savoring his tantalizing taste. His fruity, spicy fragrance mixed with her sweet floral scent to create a heady, intoxicating aroma of sensuality.

Her lips sought other areas, exploring the taste of his cheeks, then his neck, as he ravished kisses on her silken hair. Her hands roamed over the surface of his soft knit shirt until she could stand it no longer. She had to touch his skin. She slid her hands down to the hem, then plunged them beneath the fabric. Her fingertips ran along the firm muscles of his back, then around and over the crisp texture of the hairs on his chest. His body warmth seemed to intensify the already sensitive tips of her fingers as she felt the flat plane of his stomach and even stopped a moment to play with his navel.

A deep sound welled up in Randy's throat as his hands worked with the zipper at her back. His lips sent electric shivers down her spine as he kissed the sensitive area just below her ear and along her neck. They both were overwhelmed by their passion and frantic need.

Leslie felt the material of her dress slacken as Randy's deft fingers worked the zipper slowly downward. She could feel his fingers against the skin along her back as he continued his task. Once he was finished with the zipper, he eased his hand beneath the material and slipped the gown from her shoulders, making it fall down around her waist. She responded by gently pulling his shirt up over his head.

She waited until he had removed her bra before

reaching out for him again. They were both now bare to the waist, their lips once again found each other. Pressing against him, she felt the marvel of his firm, fit body against her soft, supple breasts. The texture of his hair tickled the delicate peaks as she moved her breasts across his chest. The movement seemed to arouse him even further, for he quickly stood up, pulling her with him, and pushed the black material down over her hips to let it fall to the floor. Except for her lacy panties, she stood nude before him.

"You are beautiful," he rasped, then bent down and lifted her into his arms. She put her arms willingly around his neck and nipped playfully at his ear while he made his way to her bedroom door. When they reached the closed door, she reached down to turn the knob for him and gently pushed it open.

He laid her gingerly in the soft depths of the pale-yellow comforter on her bed, removing her lace garment before he got ready to join her. She watched by the faint light drifting in through the open door, mesmerized by each movement he made while he quickly removed the rest of his clothing. When he climbed in beside her, he was just as naked and just as eager as she was.

First his lips came down to make gentle contact with hers, then he brought his body's weight down on her with agile ease. She delighted in the feel of his body naked against hers. Her hands roamed freely over the muscles of his back and strained to feel the taut muscles of his hips and upper thighs. His lightly haired skin felt good to her touch. She marveled at the fact that this man was soon to be her husband.

His hands moved to caress her shoulders first, then ran a smooth course down her sides, causing her skin to tingle with life. Slowly, he moved down so that his lips could gently caress the straining peak of one soft breast. His tongue teased the tip with short, tantalizing strokes. She arched her back eagerly, and his lips moved to take in the neglected breast.

Such sweet ecstasy—she was not certain how long she could bear it, nor was she sure how to coax him to stop this sweet torture and bring her the relief she sought. She pulled gently at his shoulders, but his mouth continued to bring her breast unbearable pleasure. She was writhing from the delectable sensations building in her, and the ache that centered itself somewhere in her abdomen was reaching unbearable intensity. Her body craved relief. "Now, Randy, love me now," she moaned, only vaguely aware that she had said the words aloud.

Drawing on first one breast, then the other, one last time, Randy moved to fulfill her, bringing their passions to an ultimate height. When the release came for Leslie, only moments before it came for Randy, it was so wondrous and shattering that she cried out with pleasure.

As the two of them sank into supreme satisfaction, she still marveled at the fact that this man, this exquisite lover, would soon be her husband. Such wondrous joys were to be hers forever.

Rolling over on top of him, aware that her breasts were dipping down to caress his chest gently, she smiled with pure love. "Do you promise it will always be like this?"

"With a beautiful wife like you for inspiration, I think it will only get better. In fact, I think I'm feeling an inspiration coming on right now."

"Don't you want to go over to Mom's and tell her our wonderful plans first?"

"If you're referring to our plans to be married, that can wait. I have other wonderful plans for us right now." Reaching up gently to grasp her head, he pulled her down for another long persuasive kiss.

As the kiss deepened, Leslie decided he was right as usual. Mom could definitely wait.

Epilogue

"Hand me those easy-to-read instructions again," Randy mumbled, putting extra emphasis on the word "easy" while frowning fiercely at the small metal washer and screw he had in his hand.

"Here you are," Leslie responded softly, trying to keep from laughing, knowing he was not going to see the humor in all this just yet. Trying to keep her expression deadpan, she reached for the large battered instruction sheet lying on the floor beside her.

"Says here that washers *e* and *f* go with screws *m* and *n* and nuts *r* and *s* to hold this piece here on the headboard. According to this illustration there are supposed to be two little holes right here," he growled, pointing to the end of a grooved board. "Now do you see any holes here? I sure don't!"

"No, I don't see any holes there," she agreed with a reassuring shake of her head. Then glancing at the illustration he had just indicated, she added sheepishly, "Maybe if your turned that board around the other way..."

Quickly examining the other end and discovering the two holes he needed, his blue eyes scanned the ceiling of the nursery as if pleading to the heavens for added strength to help see him through this. "Have you considered letting our kid sleep in a large sturdy cardboard box until he's old enough for a regular bed? We could fix it up really nice with a small mattress and everything."

Leslie flinched. She had known when she came home and found him sitting in the middle of the nursery floor mumbling to himself that it was not exactly the right time to break the news to him. She had decided to wait until he had finally gotten this baby bed together before telling him that he was going to have to put another one together. The doctor had told her today that he had definitely heard two fetal heartbeats. They were going to have twins.

"Why can't these things come already put together?" he complained, glaring at all the wooden and metal pieces scattered across the floor that still had somehow to be attached. Turning to gaze at Leslie's protruding stomach in exasperation, he leaned forward and spoke loudly, as if hoping to be heard inside. "I do hope you appreciate your old man for this."

"I'm sure they do," she assured him; then, realizing she had used plural instead of singular, she held her breath and waited for his reaction.

"Well, they'd better," he muttered, reaching for his screwdriver in order to attach the board before he could loose those two holes again. As he lined the holes up with two corresponding holes on the headboard, his

own words finally sank in. His blue eyes grew wide with
amazement, and his jaw fell limp as his gaze slowly rose
to meet hers. "They?"

Shrugging, she said, "Twins."

"Twins?"

"Twins."

"As in two?" he asked, holding up two fingers and
staring at them curiously.

"As in two."

Perplexed, he looked into her eyes a long moment
before letting his gaze drop back down to her rounded
middle. Slowly a smile stretched across his face until
his dimples carved deep hollows in his face. "Imagine
that."

"Double your pleasure." She laughed, then cautiously added, "And double your baby beds."

Suddenly his smile faded and a look of sheer horror
crossed his face. "I've got to go through all this twice? I
can't even get this one together."

"Just wait until you have to put their first swing set
together and then their first bicycles; then there will be
playhouses and gym sets..."

"All easy to assemble, I suppose," he muttered,
wondering just what he'd gotten himself into.

"Well, you wanted to be a daddy," she reminded
him.

"Yes, but I didn't know daddying was going to be so
complicated. Maybe I'm not cut out to be a daddy after
all."

"I think you'll make a wonderful daddy," she said,
scooting closer to him and kissing him reassuringly on
the cheek.

"And you are going to make a terrific mommy," he added, reaching out to give her a hug, then pulling her forward for a long, leisurely kiss. His hand roamed freely to her breast.

"Do you have to put that thing together today?" she asked, a provocative smile playing at her lips, leaving no doubt as to what she had on her mind. That kiss had put her in a very loving mood.

Quickly standing up and extending a hand to help her up from the floor, Randy grinned devilishly. "I do still have three months to figure out how to put that thing together. Maybe I'll even be able to get two of them done by then."

"Just be glad you don't have to assemble three."

As he slipped his arms around his wife and pulled her close, he considered what she had just said. "That's true, but if it does somehow turn out to be triplets, I really think we should offer your mom the pick of the litter. She's been really great through all of this."

Leslie shook her head and sighed heavily in response, but before she could openly voice a protest, Randy's lips had once again descended on hers and effectively silenced her reply. With his offbeat remark now completely forgotten, they turned toward their bedroom, still exchanging loving little kisses, secure in the realm of their love.

WORLDWIDE LIBRARY IS YOUR TICKET TO ROMANCE, ADVENTURE AND EXCITEMENT

Experience it all in these big, bold Bestsellers—Yours exclusively from WORLDWIDE LIBRARY WHILE QUANTITIES LAST

To receive these Bestsellers, complete the order form, detach and send together with your check or money order (include 75¢ postage and handling), payable to WORLDWIDE LIBRARY, to:

In the U.S.
WORLDWIDE LIBRARY
Box 52040
Phoenix, AZ
85072-2040

In Canada
WORLDWIDE LIBRARY
P.O. Box 2800, 5170 Yonge Street
Postal Station A, Willowdale, Ontario
M2N 6J3

Quant.	Title	Price
_____	**ANTIGUA KISS**, Anne Weale	$2.95
_____	**WILD CONCERTO**, Anne Mather	$2.95
_____	**STORMSPELL**, Anne Mather	$2.95
_____	**A VIOLATION**, Charlotte Lamb	$3.50
_____	**LEGACY OF PASSION**, Catherine Kay	$3.50
_____	**SECRETS**, Sheila Holland	$3.50
_____	**SWEET MEMORIES**, LaVyrle Spencer	$3.50
_____	**FLORA**, Anne Weale	$3.50
_____	**SUMMER'S AWAKENING**, Anne Weale	$3.50
_____	**FINGER PRINTS**, Barbara Delinsky	$3.50
_____	**DREAMWEAVER**, Felicia Gallant/Rebecca Flanders	$3.50
_____	**EYE OF THE STORM**, Maura Seger	$3.50
_____	**HIDDEN IN THE FLAME**, Anne Mather	$3.50
	YOUR ORDER TOTAL	$_____
	New York and Arizona residents add appropriate sales tax	$_____
	Postage and Handling	$___.75_
	I enclose	$_____

NAME _____

ADDRESS _____ APT.# _____

CITY _____

STATE/PROV. _____ ZIP/POSTAL CODE _____
WW2

Share the joys and sorrows
of real-life love with
Harlequin American Romance!™

GET THIS BOOK
FREE as your introduction to
Harlequin American Romance —
an exciting series of romance
novels written especially for
the American woman of today.

Mail to:
Harlequin Reader Service

In the U.S.
2504 West Southern Ave.
Tempe, AZ 85282

In Canada
P.O. Box 2800, Postal Station A
5170 Yonge St., Willowdale, Ont. M2N 6J3

YES! I want to be one of the first to discover
Harlequin American Romance. Send me FREE and without
obligation *Twice in a Lifetime.* If you do not hear from me after I
have examined my FREE book, please send me the 4 new
Harlequin American Romances each month as soon as they
come off the presses. I understand that I will be billed only $2.25
for each book (total $9.00). There are no shipping or handling
charges. There is no minimum number of books that I have to
purchase. In fact, I may cancel this arrangement at any time.
Twice in a Lifetime is mine to keep as a FREE gift, even if I do not
buy any additional books.   154-BPA-NAZJ

Name   (please print)

Address   Apt. no.

City   State/Prov.   Zip/Postal Code

Signature (If under 18, parent or guardian must sign.)

AMR-SUB-1

This offer is limited to one order per household and not valid to current Harlequin
American Romance subscribers. We reserve the right to exercise discretion in
granting membership. If price changes are necessary, you will be notified.

Readers rave about Harlequin American Romance!

" ...the best series of modern romances I have read...great, exciting, stupendous, wonderful."

—S.E.,* Coweta, Oklahoma

" ...they are absolutely fantastic...going to be a smash hit and hard to keep on the bookshelves."

—P.D., Easton, Pennsylvania

"The American line is great. I've enjoyed every one I've read so far."

—W.M.K., Lansing, Illinois

" ...the best stories I have read in a long time."

—R.H., Northport, New York

*Names available on request.